RUSE & ROMANCE

THE BEAUCROFT GIRLS
BOOK ONE

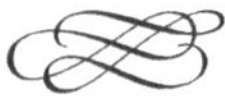

SUZANNE G. ROGERS

IDUNN COURT PUBLISHING

CONTENTS

To Robert,
My gallant hero

FLIRT

June 1845. London England

From the drawing room window, Kitty Beaucroft watched Lord Zachary Gryphon's sumptuous carriage drive off—never to return. Although she was glad he was gone, the wealthy viscount had been frightfully angry with her. If she hadn't suspected his pride had been wounded rather than his feelings, she almost would have felt sorry for him. *Undoubtedly the preening peacock expected me to weep with gratitude at his proposal of marriage.* Still, she took no pleasure in rejecting him. In fact, their short, tense conversation had left her unsettled and empty.

Moments later, her father summoned her to his study. As soon as she entered the room, she realized from the expression on his ruddy face the situation was dire. Fury crackled from his eyes, and a vein pulsed at his temple. *Oh, no!* Apprehensive, she sank into the chair facing the desk, clasped her hands on her lap, and steeled herself against the imminent storm.

"Lord Gryphon spoke with me before his departure." Mr.

Beaucroft's words were clipped. "Am I to understand you've refused his proposal of marriage?"

"Yes, sir." Kitty gulped. "He couldn't have made me happy, and—"

"I'm no longer *interested* in what will make you happy!" he thundered. "You may be one of the prettiest girls in England, but that fact has brought no benefit to this family whatsoever. Over the last two Seasons, five proposals of marriage from respectable gentlemen in possession of both titles and fortunes have come to naught. *Five!*"

A wince. "I've never lacked for suitors, Papa. Just give me a little more time to find a man with good character."

Beaucroft came out from behind his desk. Although her father was middle-aged, regular boxing and fencing had kept his athletic frame powerful. As he towered over her, Kitty's apprehension turned to naked fear.

"I've squandered a small fortune on gowns, hats, and fripperies to catch you a society husband, and I'm convinced the investment has been a poor one. After Lord and Lady Trestlebury's ball Friday night, I'm sending you off to your grandmother."

"No! Grandmama is so far away from London, I'll never see anybody!"

"I don't care. With you out of the way, your mother and I can concentrate on finding a husband for your younger sister. Due to your selfishness, poor Juliet must now live down your reputation for conceit beyond measure."

Shock straightened Kitty's spine. "That's completely unfair!"

"Fair or not, you've angered some very powerful men. Your spurned suitors will make their displeasure with you known to one and all. I'm afraid you've been branded a *flirt*."

Despite her best efforts to maintain her composure, her throat closed up and tears sprang to her eyes. "I'm sorry, Papa. I didn't mean to make trouble."

Beaucroft passed a weary hand over his face. "Let me speak plainly. If you don't reconsider your refusal of Lord Gryphon, you'll very likely never marry."

HER FACE WET WITH TEARS, Kitty sprawled on the bed while her sister sat next to her. "I can't possibly find a suitable husband now, especially if I'm branded a flirt!"

"Nobody who knows you would think you're a flirt, Kitty, but perhaps it's time to be practical. I hate to take Papa's side in this, but maybe you *should* reconsider Lord Gryphon's offer. He has a very handsome face and a fine figure. I'm not sure I've ever seen his equal."

"Yes, I understand all London is in love with the man, but appearance isn't everything. His foppish and arrogant manner sets my teeth on edge. Besides which, he took extreme umbrage at my refusal. I daresay he'd rather wed a sow than renew his addresses to me."

"Perhaps a few smiles and a bit of flattery will smooth things over."

"With any other gentleman that might suffice, but not him. Oh, Juliet, I wish Papa would allow me time to find the right man, but he's determined to send me away."

"I hope not. Although *I* shouldn't mind living with Grandmama so very much, I don't think the country would be very jolly for you...especially not when compared to town."

Kitty blotted her eyes with a handkerchief. "Maybe it's for the best. I suspect the man I'm looking for doesn't exist. I certainly haven't met him yet if he does."

"What sort of man would capture your fancy, then?"

"My ideal husband would be a gentleman of the highest character."

"A clergyman?"

"Don't be ridiculous. Given my predilection for clothes, he must be reasonably wealthy, naturally. I also want him to be active and adventuresome. I'd like him to value my opinions and ask my advice."

Her sister lowered her voice to a whisper. "And, of course, you want to look forward to going to bed with him every night."

"Juliet!" Kitty flushed pink. "Hush!"

"You needn't pretend you haven't thought about the same thing."

"Ladies aren't supposed to talk about such matters. Nevertheless, I admit I wouldn't want to be married to a man who makes my skin crawl. That rules out every fellow who has ever proposed to me, from Lord Groton to Lord Gryphon."

Juliet peered at her. "I'm beginning to wonder if you might be afraid of marriage."

"Why would you say such a silly thing?"

"You've found reasons to reject five proposals, that's why. Most girls are fortunate to receive one."

"Don't you start on me too! Papa is determined to see me wed to a man I don't love, that's all."

"He *is* angry at the moment, but Mama usually knows just the right thing to say to calm him." Juliet glanced up as Mrs. Beaucroft entered the room. "I was just telling Kitty you'll get Papa to come around."

The older woman sighed. "I'm afraid not. He and Lord Gryphon are members of the same club. Because of your refusal, the man has threatened to have him expelled. Your father is fit to be tied."

Kitty's heart sank. "Like I told you before, Juliet, it's hopeless!"

Mrs. Beaucroft sighed. "Hush, dear, and listen. You've no choice now but to accept Lord Gryphon's proposal."

"He's furious with me!"

"Write him a letter begging his forgiveness and tell him you've changed your mind."

So her choice was either to be sent away or agree to marry a man she didn't love? Although Kitty groaned inwardly, she acquiesced. "All right, Mama, but I daresay it will do no good."

She composed a letter in her best handwriting, expressing the utmost regret for her hasty refusal. Unfortunately, her letter was returned, unopened.

~

Derbyshire, England

"I simply can't believe you'd engage in fisticuffs like some sort of common Irishman!" the Marquess of Moregate exclaimed.

Philip Butler sat in an uncomfortable chair, listening while his father's angry words rained down around him like fiery hail. The bruising he'd earned the night before in a barroom brawl had blossomed into a dark splotch over his cheekbone, and his lip was swollen. Every time his father glanced at his injuries, another torrent was unleashed. Although Philip was tempted to defend his actions, he knew it would be better to let his father vent his spleen and get it over with.

At last, Moregate seemed to deflate. He sank into a chair, closed his eyes, and pinched the bridge of his nose with his thumb and forefinger.

"I've no idea what to do with you."

At last, Philip saw an opening. "Have you given any more thought to selling Grovebrook?"

"You're not going on about *that* again! I've already told you, anything I give you will necessarily be taken out of your brother's future estate! How can that possibly be fair to Augustus?"

"You know as well as I do that Grovebrook has been losing

money. Ridding yourself of the property would only increase the value of the estate."

"Let that be your brother's decision after I'm gone."

"That's too late. I'm not asking for a gift. We'll settle on a price now, and I'll pay you over a period of years out of the income. The title will remain with you until I've paid the sum in full."

The offer was so reasonable, Philip couldn't understand why his father was shaking his head. Pushed past his limit, he lost his temper. "If you don't agree to this, I swear I'll buy a *shop* to make my own living...or I'll go to America!"

Moregate blanched. "You'll do no such thing! I won't stand for a son of mine to be in trade, nor will I allow you to travel all the way across the Atlantic to live amongst brutish savages!" He gestured toward the bell pull. "Ring for a servant to fetch Augustus. This is not a discussion we should be having without him."

"Yes, sir."

Although Philip's respect for his father was immense, privately he believed his indecisiveness had contributed to the decline of the estate. Augustus had a stronger constitution, however, and Philip hoped he would take his side of things. There was always a risk he wouldn't.

When Augustus arrived, he listened while Philip pleaded his case. Afterward, he seemed perplexed. "You really needn't seek my permission to sell it, Father. If you're asking my advice, however, I think Philip has made you an excellent offer. Cut whatever price you might expect Grovebrook to fetch by thirty percent. If he's willing to pay that sum in reasonable increments, have the papers drawn up immediately."

"I knew I could count on you!" Philip pumped his brother's hand.

"Don't celebrate quite yet," Augustus said. "Grovebrook has

consistently underperformed. You do understand that if you can't make the payments, the property reverts back to Father?"

"All I'm asking for is the chance to be a landowner in my own right," Philip said. "As soon as the contract is signed, I'll leave for Grovebrook immediately."

"Not so hasty, lad," Moregate said. "I'll sell the property to you, but only if you can prove you're going to settle down."

"Settle down?" Philip frowned. "How am I supposed to do that?"

"Go to London and find a suitable society girl to marry."

A sound of disgust. "I've given up on that particular quest, remember? I've nothing to offer a society girl as a bridegroom, I've been told."

"You're not still holding a grudge against Miss Haver, are you? She's extraordinarily silly and had no right to speak to you that way," Augustus said. "Let it go."

"She did me a favor, actually. Now I know the truth of the matter, I don't have to waste my time trying to marry above my station in life."

Augustus stifled a laugh. "Now who's being silly?"

Philip's sarcasm sailed over his father's head.

"Miss Haver sold you short, Philip," Moregate said. "You're very learned *and* you possess a handsome face...when it's not covered with bruises."

"Good looks signify nothing. I'm a younger son with only a modest income and a courtesy title to my name. No girl from the Upper Ten Thousand will give me a second glance until I make something of myself."

"You shot too high with Miss Haver!" Moregate said. "You must look for a younger daughter, or perhaps a woman who is a trifle older."

"I refuse to settle, and I won't marry a girl who takes me out of desperation."

Moregate made a sound of frustration deep in his throat. "Four days hence, your cousin Eve and her husband Lord Trestlebury are giving a ball in London. Attend the affair with Augustus and mix with society. I'll consider your offer to purchase Grovebrook afterward, depending on your brother's good report of your conduct."

"But—"

"My condition is not negotiable."

"Fine, I'll go, but for you to imagine I'll find a suitable bride is a forlorn hope indeed."

He followed his brother from the room. Augustus gave him a sympathetic look.

"If no other opportunities present themselves, you can always marry Cousin Prudence."

"You're joking."

"Only a little. It all depends on how keen you are to acquire Grovebrook."

"Prudence is a fine girl to be sure, but witty conversation has never been her strong suit. How about you, Augustus? Is Father pressuring you to marry?"

"A little, but I'm rather looking forward to matrimony. I don't possess your easy gift for conversation, however, so I'm somewhat nervous about my prospects."

"Ha! With your title, fortune, and pleasant demeanor, you are certain to have your pick of beauties. Perhaps when you're engaged to the prettiest girl in London, you can persuade one of her younger sisters to marry me."

"I understand Miss Haver is still available." Augustus winked.

"Don't tease me, Augustus. If you ever inform me she's to be my sister-in-law, I'll flee to America, never to return."

London, England

EN ROUTE TO TRESTLEBURY HOUSE, the atmosphere inside the Beaucroft carriage was fraught with tension. Finally, Juliet broke the silence. "I dread these large parties. I dreamt last night my dance card stayed empty the entire evening."

"Such a dreadful occurrence is an impossibility," Kitty said. "Even though it's only your first Season, you've made your mark already. I'm surprised you haven't received a proposal yet."

Even in the dim lighting of the carriage, she could see her father's eyes narrow in her direction.

"Juliet will likely receive none until her elder sister is settled —or absent," he muttered.

Kitty bit back a retort. Despite her writing a letter of apology to Lord Gryphon, her father continued to show his displeasure with her at every turn. Tonight was her last chance. Her elaborate coiffeur and low neckline were certain to attract Gryphon's attention, but would the man listen to her apology?

She dragged herself out of a morass of self-pity long enough to admire Juliet's toilette. Her sister's lustrous light brown hair was swept up into an attractive style with cascading curls. Juliet's coloring was less dramatic than Kitty's, but it was lovely nevertheless.

"You look absolutely enchanting this evening, Juliet."

"I'm nothing compared to you, but I *am* pleased with my new gown." She smoothed the white tulle overskirt with a gloved hand.

"As you should be," Kitty said. "It's very fetching, and I can assure you, your beauty is second to none."

"And her temperament is a vast deal more pleasing than that of some other girls who shall remain nameless," Beaucroft said.

Inwardly, Kitty rolled her eyes. "Indeed it is. Juliet's sweet manners set a good example for us all, including a certain father whom I wouldn't dare identify."

Mrs. Beaucroft patted her husband's hand. "I quite agree

with Kitty. Do try to get along, dearest. Kitty has promised to do her best with Lord Gryphon tonight."

"I'll throw myself at his feet," Kitty said. "Let's hope he doesn't step on my face in the process."

She pushed the tip of her nose to one side, making her sister giggle.

"All jesting aside, Kitty, you really must avoid all appearance of scandal or impropriety tonight," Mrs. Beaucroft said. "We mustn't give anyone any additional reasons to call you a flirt."

"I'll behave myself, I promise."

AFTER KITTY and Juliet passed through the reception line at the ball, they left their parents behind amongst the throng of guests.

"Oh, look!" Juliet exclaimed. "There is Violet Haver. Would you think me frightfully rude if I left you for a few minutes? I want to ask her if she likes my gown."

Kitty gritted her teeth as she spied Miss Haver standing next to the staircase, conversing with an elderly viscount. Of all Juliet's friends, the girl was her least favorite. Although she was extraordinarily pretty, Miss Haver was a *parvenu* and a bad influence. For some inexplicable reason, her gentle sister seemed to like her company.

"Go on and enjoy yourself with your friend. I'm sure I'll find someone with whom to pass the time."

As Juliet hastened off, Lord Gryphon passed by. The man looked exceedingly dashing that evening, Kitty admitted. Not for the first time did she question her refusal of him. *Lord Gryphon and I would make a handsome couple, but something about the man seems untrustworthy.* Nevertheless, she smiled at him in an encouraging manner.

"Good evening, Lord Gryphon."

He did not acknowledge her greeting and her heart sank. *He's a lost cause, and good riddance. Can I cultivate another suitor quickly enough to placate my father? I cannot fail or tonight will be my last night in London and I'll end an old maid!*

As she moved through the crowd, several gentlemen of her acquaintance turned their backs when she met their gaze. After the fourth occurrence, real consternation ensued. *It's just a coincidence, surely.* She spoke with a few friends, but after twenty minutes, not a single one of her dances was claimed. A trickle of panic became a flood until Lord Trestlebury hastened toward her. *Oh, thank heavens! I'm saved.*

"Miss Beaucroft, do you know where I might find your sister? The dancing is about to start and I'd like her to partner me for the Promenade."

She gulped. "What a wonderful choice, Lord Trestlebury. I believe she's chatting with Miss Haver next to the main staircase."

The gentleman headed off to claim Juliet, and Kitty bit her lip. For the first time in her life, she was in grave danger of being a wallflower. When the orchestra began to warm up, she drifted into the ballroom to watch the couples assemble on the floor. Lord Gryphon's sudden appearance at her elbow gave her a start.

"Good evening, Miss Beaucroft. Do none of our London dandies suit you, or are you waiting for a duke to appear?"

She ignored the insult and gave him a flirtatious smile instead.

"Sir, I feel I owe you—"

"My friends have wagered that you won't dance more than twice tonight. I didn't take that bet because I'm rather certain you won't dance at all."

Her smile faded as she realized Gryphon and her former suitors were bent on meting out retribution for her refusals. It was no wonder she'd been ignored that evening; apparently a public humiliation had been prearranged amongst them.

"I trust that my unhappiness will afford you and your friends a great deal of satisfaction," she managed.

Gryphon was jovial. "A fair amount, I should think."

"Excuse me."

Wounded, she fled from the ballroom in search of refuge. Lady Trestlebury had given her a tour of her spacious home on a previous visit, pointing out a spare bedroom which was usually filled with out-of-season gowns. Her eyes brimming with tears, Kitty hastened down the hallway and climbed the servants' staircase to the floor above. She burst into the spare bedroom, slammed the door shut, and backed away as if pursued by the devil.

An unfamiliar male voice made her freeze. "Hullo there. I believe you have me at a disadvantage."

She whirled around to discover a half-dressed young gentleman staring at her in surprise. He was sitting in a wing chair near the window with an open book in his hands. Although he wore trousers, his well-muscled torso was bare. A squeak emerged from her throat.

"I'm so horribly sorry! Please forgive me for intruding on your privacy."

She backed toward the door. In her haste, she stepped on the train of her gown and sat down on the carpet, hard. Flushed with mortification, and upset from her exchange with Lord Gryphon, she buried her face in her hands and began to sob.

"Are you hurt?" the man asked. "Should I call a physician?"

Still sobbing, she shook her head. *Lord, strike me dead right now!*

"Come, now, it's not as bad as all that. Let's get you upright."

He gently pried her hands away from her face and coaxed her to her feet. To her relief, he'd donned a dressing gown over his trousers.

"I didn't mean to intrude, sir. I thought Lady Trestlebury used this room for storage."

"Yes, I believe the poor servants had to cart everything up to the attic before I arrived. Come sit. I can see you're shaken up."

"You're very kind, but it's not proper for me to be here." A sob caught in her throat. "Oh, what does it matter? I'm ruined anyway."

His eyes widened. "I hope not on my account?"

"Certainly not. I managed my downfall quite splendidly all on my own."

He led her to the table, where a decanter filled with amber liquid sat on a tray. After she sank into the second wing chair, he poured a glass and slid it across the polished wood.

"Drink a glass of sherry and tell me your troubles. I'm a good listener, and I'm certain your story will be a vast deal more interesting than this book."

A shudder ran through her as the wine hit the back of her throat. "Somewhat recently, I refused an offer of marriage. The fellow has been rather upset with me ever since, so tonight I tried to apologize. Instead of accepting my apology, however, he's bent on revenge."

"It seems to me your refusal of his proposal was wise."

"I agree. Unfortunately, I've made a great many similar enemies. All my former suitors are determined to see me a wallflower tonight and laugh at my comeuppance."

"Surely they will be disappointed. May I ask your name?"

"Miss Beaucroft."

"It's a pleasure to meet you, Miss Beaucroft. I'm Lord Philip Butler."

For the first time, she took a good look at him. He would have had a very handsome face if not for the yellowed bruise under his right eye, but his visage was made even more arresting by his obvious intelligence and wit. She returned his smile with one of her own.

"Why aren't you at the ball, Lord Philip? Don't you like to dance?"

"I enjoy it very much, but I've sworn off being sociable. You see, I've given up on society altogether."

A mirthless laugh. "I understand completely. In my case, however, society has given up on me." She drained her glass. "Thank you for your kindness, sir, and the wine. Now I must return to the ball and endure my punishment."

PHILIP WATCHED the lacy hem of Miss Beaucroft's gown swirl as she left. He'd intended to pass the evening alone, with only his book for company. After the door closed, however, he suddenly felt his solitude more keenly than he had before she'd arrived. Her intoxicating, lingering perfume tickled his nose, and he took a deep breath to savor the fragrance as long as possible. A chuckle escaped his lips as he remembered the shock on her face when she'd burst into his room and found it occupied. Even before she'd told him her name, he'd guessed who she was. Cousin Eve had mentioned Miss Constance Beaucroft to him and Augustus at breakfast that morning.

"Her friends call her Kitty, which I think is rather vulgar, but I've never seen a more beautiful girl. I'm sure you'll see her at the ball this evening. Augustus, you may have a good chance with her, but I warn you she's proven hard to catch."

In Philip's opinion, Miss Beaucroft was not merely beautiful, she was exquisite. He hadn't been so completely disarmed by a woman since Miss Haver. Unfortunately, there was simply no question of him successfully courting her, since she was destined to marry very well. Nevertheless, he could ensure she would at least dance tonight. The very idea that anyone would conspire to embarrass the girl was intolerable.

His valet had laid out his evening clothes in the slim chance his master might be tempted to attend the festivities. Philip stood, shrugged off his dressing gown, and reached for his freshly starched dress shirt. *I mustn't leave Miss Beaucroft unprotected amongst the wolves too long.*

GALLANTRY

*I*n the ladies' sitting room, Kitty dipped a handkerchief into some cool water and blotted the tear-stained skin around her eyes. *Perhaps if I explain the situation to Mama, she'll let me beg off the rest of the evening with a headache.* She waited as long as she dared, and then returned to the ballroom. Lord Gryphon and Miss Haver were conversing just inside the entrance, standing far too close to one another for propriety. *It didn't take long for him to begin courting another girl! His heart could not have been so very broken after all.* When the two caught sight of her, their titters sent blood rushing to her face. *May the devil take them both!*

Her mother and Juliet were occupied on the dance floor, and her father was nowhere to be seen—likely relaxing in the library with friends and a cigar. Kitty spotted Lord Trestlebury's daughter, however, and hastened to join her. The girl was scanning the ballroom, as if looking for someone, and Kitty was obliged to touch her sleeve to gain her attention.

"I must compliment you on your gown, Lady Prudence. I don't know when I've ever seen more beautiful lace."

"Thank you, Miss Beaucroft. I tatted it myself. Mama

discourages me from tatting, but I enjoy it. I don't think it's a dull pursuit in the least, do you?"

Ordinarily the subject of tatting bored Kitty senseless, but she would have talked of it for hours to avoid being left alone.

"Not at all! How many yards of lace did your gown require?"

Gryphon approached, his smile laced with venom. "I beg your pardon, Lady Prudence, but a member of my club has expressed the desire to make your acquaintance."

Without waiting for a response, he whisked Prudence away. *So I'm to be isolated as well as shunned?* Curious glances turned in her direction, but she held her head high. *I cannot let anyone see my lack of composure, or it will reflect badly on my family.* As she searched the corners of the room for some elderly, immobile companion who couldn't be coaxed away by her enemies, a dashing man stopped in front of her and bowed.

"Forgive me for being unpardonably late, Miss Beaucroft," Lord Philip said. "May I have the next dance?"

Her eyes widened. The man was impeccably dressed, his hair was groomed, and he was altogether dazzling.

"Why, it's you!" she exclaimed.

"At your service."

His kindness touched her. "You've come to the ball on my behalf, I suspect. Since you've ridden to my rescue, perhaps I should call you my gallant hero."

"I don't mind in the least. And be forewarned, I intend to dance every single dance with you if no other offers are forthcoming."

"It's highly improper, but since my reputation is already in tatters, you have my undying gratitude."

When Gryphon sidled over, Kitty bristled and quickly took Philip's arm. He immediately covered her gloved hand with his.

"Why, if it isn't my old Oxford classmate!" Gryphon's demeanor oozed insincerity. "Hello, Butler. You finally found your way to town."

"Hello, Gryphon. It's been a long time, hasn't it?" Philip's enthusiasm was noticeably contained.

"Indeed, it's been far too long. Will you join my little group in the corner? We're having a lively debate about the French, and we'd welcome your opinion."

"Thank you sir, but I must respectfully decline. Since Miss Beaucroft has promised to dance with me, I wouldn't dream of leaving her side." He lowered his voice, as if to impart a confidence. "Some despicable cad has made a nasty wager that she won't dance tonight, can you imagine? I intend to make sure he loses his money."

His plan stymied, Gryphon gave a curt bow and left in a huff. Philip merely laughed.

"You're not afraid of him?" Kitty asked. "Lord Gryphon has the ability to savage your reputation as badly as he has mine."

"I'm far too well-connected to let it bother me, and yet too low on the social ladder to have it signify one way or the other. I thank you, however, for your concern."

Kitty glanced at her dance card. "A waltz is next."

"I hope the room is prepared to take notice of us." Wink.

Philip led her out onto the floor. As they danced, he was a graceful and assured partner, and it pleased her to no end his eyes never fixed themselves on her décolleté, despite the fact her mother had insisted she wear a gown with a scandalously low neckline.

"After our dance we must arrange to be properly introduced, I think," she said.

"I'll ask Lady Trestlebury to do the honors. She's my second cousin."

His cousin? Lord Philip is well-connected, then, but is he wealthy enough to please Papa? Before she could devise another probing question, Philip asked one of his own.

"I don't mean to be indelicate, but was Gryphon one of your rejected suitors, perchance?"

"You already know the answer. You've also properly surmised he was the architect of my humiliation this evening."

"You're well rid of the man, I must say. Be assured, you have nothing to fear from him while I'm around."

"Thank you." *Not only is he perceptive, but his eyes crinkle at the corners when he smiles.* "You're very kind."

AS HE WALTZED with Miss Beaucroft, Philip noticed onlookers craning their necks to get a better look. Were they speculating about the identity of the young gentleman who was dancing with the most beautiful girl in the room? Even now, guests were clustered around Lord Trestlebury, making comments as they stared. Scuttlebutt and gossip were sure to follow. Although he hoped their conversations were kind, he knew better.

He spied his cousin Eve, chatting with Augustus next to a potted plant. When the last strains of the waltz faded away, Philip escorted his partner over for a formal introduction. As they drew near, Augustus fixed his gaze on Miss Beaucroft. Philip was amused to see the smitten look on his brother's face. He'd had the same awestruck expression on his thirteenth birthday, when presented with his first full-sized horse.

Eve beamed. "There you are, Miss Beaucroft! My cousin Augustus has just expressed a desire to meet you. Allow me to introduce Lord Elbourne. He's the eldest son of the Marquess of Moregate, dear."

Miss Beaucroft curtsied. "It's a pleasure, Lord Elbourne."

"The pleasure is mine. I was dancing with your sister a little earlier, and she spoke of you quite highly."

"Juliet is very kind."

"I see you've already met Lord Elbourne's younger brother, Lord Philip Butler." Eve unconsciously delivered the last sentence in a dismissive fashion, as if Philip couldn't possibly matter.

"Thanks, cousin. The heir and the spare," he quipped.

Another curtsy, although Miss Beaucroft slipped Philip a mischievous smile as she rose.

"Miss Beaucroft, might I reserve a dance?" Augustus asked.

"Indeed, sir, you may. I arrived late to the ball and so my dance card is completely open. Your gallant brother offered to keep me company."

Augustus' pointed glance was designed to get Philip to leave. "Awfully kind of you, old chap."

"Not at all." Philip bit back a laugh.

"The orchestra is returning." Augustus offered his arm to Miss Beaucroft. "Shall we?"

"I would be honored."

As his brother led Miss Beaucroft away, she gave Philip an almost imperceptible wink. Eve leaned in closer to Philip. "You'd do better to concentrate your efforts where they'll be appreciated, cousin. I'd suggest Prudence, but I know you better than that. Besides which, her father is determined to see her marry very well." A line of worry creased her forehead. "I wish he would realize that his ambition is getting in the way of his daughter's happiness."

"Ambition is a two-edged sword, I'm afraid."

"Indeed it is, and Prudence is in grave danger of becoming a spinster if he doesn't stop meddling." She patted his arm. "May I introduce you to Miss Juliet? If Augustus intends to pursue Miss Beaucroft, it will matter much less whom her younger sister weds."

His cousin meant well, so Philip covered his annoyance. "Please don't trouble yourself. I think you've misinterpreted the situation. Although Miss Beaucroft is admittedly quite charming, I'm perfectly content as a bachelor."

"If you say so. Enjoy the ball!"

Eve disappeared from view in the crowd. Philip suddenly realized Miss Haver had taken her place at his side. Since she must have been standing very near, she could not have failed to overhear the entire conversation.

"Good evening, Miss Haver." Although he tried to keep the ice from his voice, the best he could achieve was decidedly cool.

She batted her long inky black eyelashes. "Good evening, Lord Philip. I see you've met the famous Miss Beaucroft. I admire your lofty aspirations."

"My aspirations are not as lofty as yours, Miss Haver, but I thank you for the compliment."

With a faint, mocking smile, he bowed and took his leave. He strode from the ballroom, in search of a stiff drink before retiring. To his pleasant surprise, a familiar face—Lord Frederick Kirkham—had just arrived at the ball and was relinquishing his hat and coat to a servant.

"Kirkham!" Philip exclaimed. "This is a surprise."

They shook hands.

His friend peered at Philip's face. "Did you get that bruise fighting over a girl?"

A chuckle. "After a fashion. I was in a tavern a few miles from home and overheard some lout insulting the barmaid. I respectfully suggested the fellow apologize, but he declined. In the end, I guarantee he regretted his ungentlemanly behavior."

"Was the barmaid good-looking?"

"Probably not. To be honest, I was too drunk to notice one way or another, but I couldn't let the insult pass."

Boisterous laughter. "You're such a romantic! Champion of long shots, ladies, and dark horses."

"You think so? And here I was, worried I was becoming a cynic. Join me for a drink?"

"Don't mind if I do."

ALTHOUGH JULIET TRIED to mask her envy, it was difficult to watch Lord Elbourne dancing with Kitty with such obvious enjoyment. When Miss Haver joined her, she followed Juliet's gaze.

"Ah, I see Lord Elbourne has wiggled off your hook in favor of your sister. Does she ever tire of stealing everyone else's suitors, I wonder?"

"It's not Kitty's fault men are drawn to her."

"Only because she's a flirt. *You* were the belle of the ball until she took the floor with Lord Philip Butler and drew everyone's attention to her."

Juliet couldn't deny that she *had* felt like the belle of the ball...for a little while, anyway. Nevertheless, she decided to change the subject before she gave voice to her feelings.

"Who is Lord Philip Butler?" she asked. "I noticed him dancing with Kitty, but we've not been introduced."

"He's Lord Elbourne's younger brother, and therefore no one at all."

"Pity. He's dreadfully handsome."

"I suppose so. He was besotted with me, but I discouraged his attentions."

"Why?"

"He has no money to speak of. It's his brother who is the prize."

Juliet glanced at her friend. "You speak as if he's sparked your interest."

"Oh, no, I think of him only for you."

Lord Elbourne and Kitty floated past on the dance floor. The elegant earl was seemingly transfixed by her beauty, and Juliet bit her lip in frustration.

Violet gave Juliet a sad smile. "I'm sorry."

"What do you mean?"

"Lord Elbourne, of course. You and he danced so well together. Perhaps your sister will cast him off as she has every other eligible gentleman in London, and you may renew your acquaintance once more."

A frown tugged at Juliet's lips. *I do love Kitty, but it's so tiresome always taking crumbs from her table. Papa is right; if she were settled, I'd have no trouble at all catching a suitable beau for myself.* Frustrated, she turned her back on the dancers.

"Violet, let's get a cup of punch. I'm thirsty."

WHEN KITTY'S dance with Lord Elbourne came to an end, he escorted her off the floor and sketched a bow.

"I regret having to leave you for a little while, but I promised the next dance to my cousin Prudence."

"Lady Prudence is a lovely girl, and quite talented with lace."

"Really? I must ask her about that."

Kitty was pleased when he signed her card for two more dances toward the end of the evening. He hurried away, and she was at loose ends once more. Although she glanced around for Lord Philip, he was nowhere to be found. To avoid scrutiny, she decided to wander the garden pathways for a little while. She made her way out of the house, down the steps, and into the cool of the night. Twenty paces later, she heard Lord Gryphon call her name.

"Miss Beaucroft! Please wait."

Oh, dear. Her first instinct was to flee into the darkness as quickly as possible, but she was afraid of tripping on her gown and landing in a bed of thorns. She paused, and a few moments later, Gryphon joined her. Moonlight made his eyes glitter and his teeth gleam.

"Will you walk a bit with me?"

"No." She glanced back toward the house to see if they were observed. "It's not proper."

"Please, Miss Beaucroft. Your father has given me his permission to speak with you."

"Did he?" Ordinarily, Kitty would have dismissed the assertion as nonsense. Considering her father's desire for her to secure Lord Gryphon, however, he might very well indeed have brushed propriety aside and given his permission. "All right, but just for a little while."

They headed down the path. The farther they went from the house, the more uncomfortable Kitty became. Finally, she stopped and edged backward.

"It's rather dark here. Perhaps we should turn around."

He caught her hand so she couldn't leave. "Forgive me for my earlier pique. I should not have spoken nor acted thusly. Please accept my apologies."

"Such revenge *was* unworthy of you, especially since I've been trying to tender my most sincere apologies for having given offense."

"I take it you'd like me to renew my offer?"

Her instinct was to tell him no in the loudest voice possible, but she hesitated. Her father's admonitions echoed in the back of her mind. Surely when she told him about Lord Gryphon's behavior, he wouldn't blame her for her refusal.

Gryphon must have taken her silence for assent, because he stepped closer. His gaze went to her cleavage, and the tip of his tongue ran along his upper lip. "Your charms are on full display this evening."

Kitty masked her revulsion. "Thank you. Let us take the shortest way back to the house."

When she brushed past him, his hands shot out and she found herself pinned in a tight grip.

"Let go!"

"You've made a fool of me, Miss Beaucroft. Now I mean to sample your goods."

As Philip and Kirkham sipped their glasses of wine at a back table in the banquet room, two young ladies entered and headed for the punch bowl.

"Oh, look…Miss Haver is here." Kirkham scrunched up his face in mock terror. "I can't believe you ever found her attractive. She encouraged you abominably, only to set you down. A streak of cruelty lays hidden behind her green eyes."

"I was young, naïve, and impressionable at the time."

"The girl accompanying Miss Haver has a sweet air about her. I wonder if she has any idea about her friend's true nature?"

"Doubtless the poor girl will discover her mistake too late, like I did. I owe Miss Haver one debt of gratitude, however. I now have a goal for myself that doesn't include marriage."

"That's right! Have you made any progress in your quest to secure Grovebrook?"

"Yes and no. My brother has endorsed the sale, but my father isn't convinced. He wants me to settle down first."

"Settle down?" Kirkham seemed confused. "So…you're on the hunt for a wife?"

"Not hardly, but if Augustus tells Father I'm making an effort, I may yet prevail. That's why I came with him to London."

Kirkham laughed and held up his glass for a toast. "Here's to matrimony."

"Matrimony?" A sidelong glance. "You have your eye on a lady?"

"Alas, I'm smitten, but she's far above me in every way. I'm only a penniless viscount and she's the daughter of an exceedingly wealthy earl."

"A Herculean task, then, I grant you. Might I ask the name of the lady who has captivated your fancy?"

"In fact, it's your cousin Prudence."

"Really? Does she return your affection?"

"We've not discussed our feelings openly, but I believe she may." He sighed. "It's a hopeless situation, I fear. Lord Trestlebury would certainly take a dim view of our courtship, if he knew."

Philip didn't want to dash his friend's hopes, but he didn't feel it was proper to encourage him overmuch in the face of impossible odds.

"You're a worthy gentleman, Kirkham, but I'm afraid you're right. Nevertheless, I'd like to see you happy. I wish you the best of luck."

"Thank you. To paraphrase Virgil, may love conquer all!"

Kirkham strode from the banquet room, his shoulders squared as if going into battle. Philip finished his wine, and then wandered out a side door and onto the grounds. The darkness swallowed him whole, and he sank down on a cold granite bench in the garden to stare up at the stars. *I'm too romantic, am I?* He shrugged. *Maybe so.*

His thoughts turned to Miss Beaucroft. Despite their rather scandalous beginning—or perhaps because of it—he liked her. It was more than her considerable good looks that had attracted him. He found her indomitable spirit and plucky attitude very appealing. Her rejection of Gryphon meant she had good taste and judgment, too. Augustus had certainly made his interest obvious. Would his brother be the fortunate swain to finally capture her heart?

The sound of raised voices reached his ears and raised his hackles.

"You've no right to touch me that way!" a woman exclaimed.

A man's voice replied, "If you don't want to be my wife, perhaps you'd enjoy the role of mistress."

"Let me pass, I beg you!"

"Relax, Miss Beaucroft. You might find you like it."

Miss Beaucroft? Philip hastened toward the voices, finally spotting the couple struggling with one another next to a clump of rose bushes. He strode over.

"Gryphon, you're not imposing yourself on respectable young ladies again, are you? I thought you'd given all that up."

The man whirled around, clearly annoyed at the interruption. "Run along, Philip, and tilt at windmills."

"Why don't you slither underneath a rock first?" Philip shot back. "Step away from the lady before I'm forced to set you down."

Miss Beaucroft's hair was disheveled, and her gown had slipped off one shoulder.

"Lord Philip! Will you escort me back to the house?" The desperation in her voice was evident.

Philip maneuvered himself between Miss Beaucroft and her assailant. "Indeed, I would like nothing better."

Undeterred, Gryphon bristled. "Leave now, if you value your skin."

"Unlike you, I value honor and integrity more than my skin. You're a bully, Gryphon. And if it weren't for your father's intervention, you would've been expelled from Oxford for being a cheat."

"How dare you insult me!" The man's eyes narrowed. "You'll regret it, I promise you that."

Philip took Miss Beaucroft by the hand and pulled her toward the house. They were almost to safety when she hesitated. "You go on ahead. I must compose myself or everyone will know something is wrong. I must avoid a scandal at all costs."

"I can't leave you alone out here." He spied a gardener's shed. "Come on."

Although the spacious shed was dark and smelled like earth, it afforded Miss Beaucroft privacy. He turned his back while she adjusted her clothes and smoothed her hair.

"Do I look all right?" she asked finally.

The moonlight shining through the shed windows gave her the appearance of an angel, but he didn't say so.

"Shipshape," he said. "May I ask how you came to be alone with that scoundrel?"

"He followed me into the garden. I should have returned to the house right away, but he said my father gave him permission to speak with me. I thought if I refused, my father would be furious."

"Why?"

"You wouldn't understand. Your father has probably never asked you to do something you didn't want to do."

"You might be surprised. Try me."

A sigh. "After I rejected Lord Gryphon's proposal, my father threatened to send me to my grandmother's house in the country. I've been labeled a flirt, you see, and my younger sister may be tainted by association."

"We've just met, but I don't think you're a flirt."

"Thank you. I've only ever wanted to marry a gentleman whom I cared for deeply. I haven't met him yet, and now I've run out of time. I think I shall *die* cloistered so far away from London!"

"I understand a little more than you might think. You're expected to sell yourself to the highest bidder, even if it's a lout like Gryphon. As for me, my father has agreed to sell me some property, but only if I seem to be settling down. By some miracle I'm supposed to find a society girl who is desperate enough to marry the younger son of a marquess. These circumstances are not of our making, are they?"

"No. Perhaps you do understand me after all."

"If you're ready, we should go." Philip ushered Miss Beaucroft from the shed. "Now, take this path back to the house, slip through a side door, and say nothing of this to anyone. I'll return by way of the garden stairs."

"You're a true gentleman."

After she gave him an impulsive kiss on the cheek—which he felt all the way to his toes—she hastened off. After he'd recovered from his surprise, he took a more circuitous route through the garden. When he was a few yards from the garden stairs, Gryphon and two of his friends hastened forward out of the shadows. Philip recognized the newcomers as Lord Groton and Mr. Miller, whom he knew to be arrogant and churlish.

An ugly frown distorted Gryphon's features. "You're going to pay for your interference."

Philip chuckled. "Three against one? This just might be a fair fight."

SCURRILOUS LIES

itty assumed a serene expression before slipping through a side door and into the banquet room. The dancing had given way to the supper part of the evening, and tables were filled with guests. As she surveyed the crowd, looking for her parents or Juliet, a shout from the hallway caused an excited commotion. Although she tried to make out what was being said, the babble made no sense. Shortly thereafter, people began to rush from the room. She caught sight of Lord Elbourne as he brushed past.

"What is happening, sir?" she asked.

"There's a brawl in the garden."

"Oh, no!"

"Yes, and where there's brawling, I'm fairly certain my brother must be in the midst of it. Excuse me, Miss Beaucroft, while I intervene." He hastened off.

Kitty joined the exodus from the ballroom and pushed her way through the crowd. As she looked down into the garden from the railing, her worst fears were realized. Two men were holding Philip by either arm while Lord Gryphon was assaulting him with his fists.

"Stop that this instant!" she exclaimed.

Gryphon paused at the sound of her voice. A gentleman who'd just bounded down the stairs spun him around and clocked him with a punch to his mouth. Gryphon staggered to one side, but as he lunged forward again, Elbourne stepped in to block his momentum.

"That's enough! This is over."

Juliet arrived at Kitty's elbow. "What on earth is happening?"

The men holding Philip let him go, and he sank to his knees, dazed. Although he'd clearly received the worst of it, his assailants had bloodied noses and black eyes. Gryphon had also just sustained a freshly cut lip.

His knuckles bleeding, Philip's defender knelt next to him. "Are you all right, Butler?"

"Thanks, Kirkham. I'm just a little winded," Philip managed.

Elbourne pulled his brother to his feet.

"Kirkham, kindly help me take Philip to his room, please."

"Of course."

They each draped one of Philip's arms across their shoulders, and as they assisted him into the house, the crowd parted to let them pass. Moments later, Lord Trestlebury arrived with a retinue of servants who whisked Gryphon and the other injured men away to tend to their wounds.

"I wonder why Lord Gryphon and Lord Philip were fighting?" Juliet asked.

"I-I don't know, but everybody seems to be wondering the same thing," Kitty replied.

The excitement over, the crowd filtered back into the banquet room, where Lady Trestlebury was wringing her hands and lamenting the ruination of her soirée. Although Kitty understood the woman's distress, the guests appeared to be more vitalized than before the fight began. To her dismay, many whispers and sidelong looks seemed to be directed at Kitty. A self-conscious hand went to smooth her coiffeur. *Is it because I shouted at Lord Gryphon or is my hair still mussed from his assault?*

Her father approached, his eyes narrowed. "We're leaving."

Certainly Kitty felt no pressing need to remain at the ball, not since both Lord Elbourne and Lord Philip had so obviously retired for the night. For Juliet's sake, however, she was surprised at her father's dour attitude.

"Why?"

"Gossip has it Lord Gryphon and Lord Philip were engaging in fisticuffs over you."

Kitty gulped, hoping guilt wasn't written on her face. "How could anyone arrive at that conclusion?"

"Because your rejection of Lord Gryphon is well known, and you're the only lady Lord Philip danced with tonight."

As the Beaucroft carriage sped through the shadowy streets of London, the closed compartment made Kitty feel like a mouse in a matchbox.

"Why does scandal seem to follow wherever you go?" her father demanded.

"It's just idle gossip." Shame heated her face, and she was grateful for the concealing darkness.

"You mustn't leap to conclusions, Papa," Juliet said.

"Am I correct in assuming you did not mend your relationship with Lord Gryphon?" Beaucroft asked.

Kitty dared not tell him the complete truth of the matter. "I tried, but the man is contemptible. He insulted me in every possible way!"

Mrs. Beaucroft tried to keep the peace. "Lord Elbourne took notice of her, dearest. He's to inherit the title of Marquess someday."

"Yes, that's no small victory," Beaucroft admitted. "The earl's younger brother, on the other hand, has a reputation as a ne'er do well and a ruffian."

"Many society gentlemen have a reputation for wildness before they settle down," Kitty said.

"He was brawling!"

Juliet cleared her throat. "As were Lord Gryphon, Lord Groton, and Mr. Miller. It seemed to me, however, Lord Philip was being beaten."

"He was!" Kitty exclaimed. "Lord Philip and I got along famously earlier. I like him very much indeed."

"You may as well forget about him," Beaucroft said. "He's unsuitable by any standard, and tonight's debacle proves it."

"There must have been a very good reason for his fight with Lord Gryphon," Juliet said. "Perhaps there was some bad blood between them and it had nothing to do with Kitty whatsoever."

"Be that as it may, tonight's scandalous and public brawl has once again made our eldest daughter the focus of salacious gossip," Beaucroft said.

"Exactly the opposite of everything we're trying to achieve," Mrs. Beaucroft added.

"The notion I had anything to do with it is absurd," Kitty managed.

"Absurd or not, the damage is done," Beaucroft said. "Due to Lord Elbourne's marked interest in you this evening, however, I'll allow three days for him to call. If he doesn't, you'll be packed off to my mother, forthwith."

"And we'll try to salvage the rest of Juliet's Season as best we can," Mrs. Beaucroft said.

The carriage fell silent. Forlorn, Kitty stared out the window, where a misty fog was pressing against the glass. Gryphon had proven himself to be the worst sort of person. He'd intended to take liberties and leave her in the garden without dignity or a marriage proposal. Thank heavens Lord Philip had been passing by! The memory of him, battered and bleeding, suddenly flashed into her mind. She squeezed her eyes shut, wishing someone could give her assurance he would be all right. When she sent a note of thanks to Lady Trestlebury in the morning, she would inquire after his health and express a sincere hope for his speedy recovery.

IN THE MORNING, Augustus went to Philip's room to check on his condition. His brother's body was covered with bruises, and he was struggling unsuccessfully to rise. In addition, he'd suffered a black eye and a cut over his cheekbone.

"What a mess." Augustus sighed. "Three against one was badly done."

"Don't forget, Kirkham got a lick in at the end."

"Be that as it may. Can you tell me what the fight was about?"

Philip waved his hand, dismissively. "The usual. Too much wine and too many insults."

"I find that difficult to believe." Augustus chose his next words carefully. "If you don't speak, your reticence will allow Gryphon to make up any story he likes."

"He can have nothing to say that won't reflect badly on him."

"We're members of the same club. If you tell me the real reason, I'll say a word on your behalf when I'm there for lunch today."

"I've told you already and there's nothing more to add."

"All right. Why don't you rest for a while longer? I'll ask Eve to send up a tray."

"You have my gratitude."

Puzzled at his brother's reluctance to confide in him, Augustus left the room and continued downstairs to breakfast. As he entered the dining room, he said good morning to Eve, Trestlebury, and Prudence.

"Philip is somewhat incapacitated this morning and won't be down for breakfast," Augustus said. "He conveys his apologies."

"Poor fellow," Prudence said.

"Oh, dear. I'll have a tray of soft foods sent up." Eve gestured to one of the servants to see to it. "The physician assured me there was no lasting harm from his injuries."

"No, but he's rather uncomfortable."

"A drop of laudanum will prove efficacious," Trestlebury said. "It does wonders for my aches and pains."

"I believe the physician left a bottle on the nightstand," Eve said.

Augustus nodded. "Yes, I recall seeing it when I was in Philip's room just now."

He noticed a pile of letters stacked on a tray next to his cousin's plate.

"So much correspondence first thing in the morning must mean the ball was a great success."

Eve gloated over the letters. "I was of a mind to be greatly vexed at Philip for his lack of self-control, but apparently the *contretemps* was red meat to the lions. All my friends found the brawl rather exciting."

"Why blame it entirely on Philip?" Prudence asked. "My recollection is that Lord Gryphon, Lord Groton, and Mr. Miller were involved."

"And Lord Kirkham," Trestlebury interjected. "He couldn't wait to wade into the fray, I'm told."

"It was a good thing Lord Kirkham did intervene," Prudence shot back. "His heroics saved Philip from another blow."

"When it's all said and done, my brother has a well-deserved reputation for being hot-headed, I'm afraid," Augustus said. "Father is hoping marriage will settle him down."

"Has Philip mentioned what started the fight?" Trestlebury asked.

"He passed it off as having imbibed too much, but I feel as if there's more to it."

Eve gestured toward the opened correspondence. "The gossips believe the fight between Philip and Lord Gryphon was over Miss Beaucroft."

Augustus was taken aback. "I can't imagine why. Did Gryphon say that?"

"Not directly, but everyone is aware of her somewhat surprising rejection of his proposal. Furthermore, I detected a partiality toward Miss Beaucroft on Philip's part." Her glance fell onto one of the newly arrived envelopes. "Aha! Here's a note from the lady herself."

Her eyes darted back and forth as she read the neat, feminine handwriting inscribed thereon.

"All the usual compliments about the evening, of course, but she ends by inquiring after Lord Philip's health." She giggled and exchanged a conspiratorial glance with her husband.

"Certainly adds fuel to the fire," he said.

"I had intended to call on Miss Beaucroft this afternoon," Augustus said. "I'll let her know he's on the mend."

Eve beamed with satisfaction. "Aha! I suspected Miss Beaucroft might catch your eye."

Augustus suppressed a smile. "Actually, it was Miss Juliet who drew my admiration at first."

"The Beaucroft girls are quite lovely," Prudence said. "I've no doubt both will marry well."

AUGUSTUS ARRIVED at his gentlemen's club on Pall Mall by carriage. Many months had passed since he'd had the opportunity to visit, and he was looking forward to chatting with friends and having lunch. No sooner had he'd settled down in a wing chair with a newspaper, when he overheard his brother's name mentioned in nearby conversation.

"Lord Philip Butler certainly got himself a good thrashing at the Trestlebury ball last night."

"I wasn't there, but to hear Lord Gryphon tell the tale, the argument happened because he stopped Butler from taking liberties with Miss Beaucroft."

"No, not really!"

"That's his story. If it's not true, let the lady refute it. Unfortunately for Butler, Gryphon has witnesses to back him up."

"Who, Groton and Miller? Those two reprobates might be counted upon to say anything for the price of a stiff drink."

"Indeed, but not everyone will see it that way."

"I never took Butler for a rake."

"No, but perhaps the beautiful Miss Beaucroft brought out the wolf in him."

Uproarious laughter followed the remark. Past annoyed, Augustus folded up his newspaper, stood, and confronted the gentlemen.

"Excuse me for interrupting, but Lord Philip Butler is my younger brother and a member in good standing of this club. He's neither a rake nor a libertine."

The men looked stricken.

"I say, Lord Elbourne, no offense meant," the eldest one said. "You should know, however, I've heard the same story from several different sources. It's all London is talking of."

"Circulating such gossip is beneath you, sir. It seems Lord Gryphon is spreading malicious rumors for unsavory reasons of his own. I can assure you, I'll get to the bottom of it."

His appetite for lunch gone, Augustus left the club and visited his tailor instead. While he was being fitted for a new suit, he stewed over what he'd heard. Gryphon's version of events made no sense at all and was undoubtedly self-serving.

When I tell Philip what's being said, he cannot fail to speak on his own behalf.

~

ALTHOUGH KITTY TRIED to distract herself with a book, her anxiety rose as the day wore on. Would Lord Elbourne call on her that afternoon or was it too soon? More importantly, Lady Trestlebury hadn't yet replied to her inquiry regarding Lord Philip's health. Despite the protestations she'd made to the contrary, Kitty believed Gryphon had attacked Philip for defending her, and his condition weighed on her mind like a millstone.

Juliet made it even more difficult to concentrate due to her lengthy and persistent practice on the piano. She played as if possessed by a hummingbird, and finally Kitty begged her to leave off.

"I know, let's walk to the park." She lowered her voice. "I feel as if I'm suffocating."

Juliet's eyes darted toward her mother, who sat next to a window embroidering a screen.

"May we have permission to go to the park, Mama?"

"Yes, but one of the maids must come with you as a chaperone. This family needs no further scandal."

After retrieving their hats and gloves, Kitty and Juliet stepped out of the house. They walked toward Hyde Park, with Kitty's maid, Bridget, following several yards behind.

Kitty inhaled and blew out her breath in a gust. "Finally, a tiny bit of freedom. I thought I would scream if I stayed indoors another moment."

Juliet glanced at her. "Something is bothering you, I can tell. Would it have something to do with how your hair became so mussed last night?"

"Was it that noticeable?"

"Only to me. I watched Bridget arrange your hair just so, remember? And you've got little bruises on your wrists and arms that weren't there yesterday."

"I give you credit for your powers of observation." Kitty tugged her gloves higher on her wrists to cover the petal bruises. "It was quite a horrible scene, actually. I took a turn in the garden with Lord Gryphon last night—"

"Alone?"

"He lied and told me Papa gave him permission to speak with me. Anyway, he'd been beastly earlier in the evening and said he wanted to apologize. Then he...he attempted to take liberties."

Juliet's jaw dropped. "What?"

"I tried my best to get away, but he wouldn't let me go. The only thing that saved my honor was the timely intervention of Lord Philip, and I suspect that's what led to the brawl."

"Merciful heavens. You must tell Papa!"

"Absolutely not! If Papa found out, he'd have me drawn and quartered for shaming the family. Then he'll ship whatever is left to Grandmama. You'd have to carry on in the shadow of my infamy."

"But it's not your fault Lord Gryphon tried to impose himself on you."

"In the world we live in, it's always the girl's fault, Juliet. I believed his lie and went off with him, willingly."

"I'm embarrassed to have been led astray by Lord Gryphon's angelic looks. He's not at all handsome underneath the surface. What will you do?"

"I've no choice but to pretend nothing ever happened. Lord Philip is too much of a gentleman to reveal my secret, and if Lord Gryphon should speak of it, I'll deny everything. He'll be regarded as a cad and a scoundrel."

"You're greatly in Lord Philip's debt."

"Indeed I am."

"If you marry Lord Elbourne, nobody will hold anything against you."

"Yes. I do hope he comes to call." For her sister's sake, Kitty feigned enthusiasm. Her feelings for Lord Elbourne were far from passionate. Nevertheless, she was determined to do the proper thing for her family—Juliet in particular. If a marriage of convenience was in her future, so be it.

"Lord Elbourne asked to be introduced to me last night," Juliet said. "We danced together."

"Yes, he mentioned that to me. Do you like him?"

"He's wonderful. As soon as he saw you, however, his interest in me waned."

Kitty stole a glance at Juliet's downcast expression. "Oh, no. I hope you're not too disappointed?"

"Perhaps a little, but it can't be helped."

As MIDDAY APPROACHED, Philip felt a great deal more restored. After he'd dressed, he sought out Eve to explain (as much as he could without involving Miss Beaucroft) his part in the melee. Unfortunately, everyone in the family was gone. Augustus and Trestlebury were lunching at their respective clubs, and Eve and Prudence had been invited to lunch with friends. Philip had a bite to eat alone in the dining room and then went into the library to seek out something interesting to read.

Kirkham came to call in the afternoon. The butler showed him into the library, where Philip greeted him with pleasure. They shook hands, even as Kirkham winced in sympathy at Philip's injuries.

"You've looked better, I must say."

"Indeed I have. You got off a round and came off unscathed," Philip replied.

"Not quite." Kirkham flashed his bruised and lacerated knuckles.

"Sorry. I certainly hope Gryphon isn't rabid."

"Ha! I'm not taking bets on that. Three against one was certainly poor form. What the devil came over Gryphon?"

"Gryphon *is* a devil, if truth be known."

"If that's the case, then Groton and Miller are his minions."

They laughed.

"I couldn't agree more. Why was Gryphon pounding you?"

"He and I never got along at Oxford, as you know, and things between us have not improved. One thing led to another, I suppose."

Kirkham's grin was wry. "A lady is involved, obviously, and you're protecting her. I've always liked your style." He paused. "Is the family at home?"

"Everyone's gone out, I'm afraid." Philip chuckled. "How are things coming along with Prudence?"

"Quite well, actually, but I don't like being underhanded. I'd hoped to see Lord Trestlebury today, to test the waters."

"What will you do if he forbids the match?"

"Prudence and I might elope."

Philip frowned. "I hope not. She deserves better than to be stolen away in the middle of the night."

"Yes…quite so." His shoulders drooped. "Prudence deserves far better."

"Think carefully before you act, and never forget you're a gentleman. Whatever your decision, it ought to be the proper thing for Prudence."

He nodded. "Agreed."

"If there's ever anything I can do, let me know. I feel as if I owe you a debt of gratitude for defending me last night."

"Thank you, my friend, but I'm sure you would have done the same for me."

Kirkham took his leave. Philip had no sooner settled into a

chair with his book when Augustus appeared. His brother wore an uncharacteristically grim expression.

"Is something amiss?" Philip asked.

"A report of an alarming nature has surfaced, involving you and Miss Beaucroft."

Baffled, Philip stared. "I'm sorry, but I've no idea to what you may be referring."

"Lord Gryphon has let it be known why his encounter with you came to blows. According to him, he prevented you from imposing yourself on her."

Shock made Philip gasp. "That's a bald-faced lie!"

"Furthermore, he claims it required him, Lord Groton, and Mr. Miller to dissuade you from compromising the lady's virtue."

"A complete fabrication in every regard! I would never treat a woman so."

"I believe you, Philip, but this is serious. You must tell me the truth if I'm to help."

"I..." Philip trailed off, in a quandary. If he admitted to seeing Miss Beaucroft alone with Gryphon, her reputation would be compromised irreparably, but the alternative would be to compromise his own.

"What I'm about to divulge is in the strictest confidence. I do so only because it pains me for you to have any doubts as to my character. Have I your word as a gentleman and my brother that you won't speak of it to anyone?"

Augustus nodded. "You do."

"The truth is, Gryphon lured Miss Beaucroft to the garden with the intent of taking liberties. I happened upon them as he was forcing his attentions on her and intervened so she could return to the house. He took umbrage at my interference, and is now seeking to revenge himself upon me with his scurrilous tale."

"You must speak out, Philip, or be branded a bounder!"

"I can't. To do so would be to put Miss Beaucroft in an irretrievably unflattering light. This I won't do."

"Not even to save your own skin?"

"Not even then."

Augustus passed his hand over his face, clearly nonplussed. "Your chivalry does you credit, but as your elder brother, I can't allow you to take the blame for Gryphon's transgressions."

"Miss Beaucroft will refute the story and all will be well."

"She may do so, but Gryphon has two additional witnesses—Groton and Miller—on his side."

"Nobody will believe them. They're idiots."

"You and I must call on the Beaucrofts this afternoon, and hear Miss Beaucroft's version of events before we decide how to proceed."

"I've no doubt—none whatsoever—the lady will gladly clear my name." Philip paused. "She's blameless in this business, Augustus. I hope this won't affect your good opinion of her."

"Of course not, but I'm wondering how Gryphon could have lured her to the garden alone. Is it possible she's still besotted with him?"

"No. She was almost fearful of him earlier in the evening."

"He may have overstepped the mark, but that doesn't mean she didn't encourage him to begin with."

"Nonsense."

Augustus pursed his lips. "Truthfully, I don't know enough about the situation to draw a reasonable conclusion."

"I wish now I'd hit Gryphon twice as hard."

THE RUSE

After returning from the park with her sister, Kitty went to her room to change into a tea gown with full lacy sleeves long enough to cover her wrists. She'd just finished her toilette when she heard her father's voice from downstairs, bellowing her name. Alarmed, she opened the door to the hallway.

"Coming, Papa!"

Her sister emerged from her bedchamber. "What's wrong?"

Wide-eyed, Kitty shook her head. "I've no idea what I've done, but Papa sounds angry!"

Their mother met them on the stairs, having descended from the floor above. "Why is your father shouting for you, Kitty?"

"I don't know." She gulped. "Perhaps something untoward happened at his club today?"

Mrs. Beaucroft shooed her along. "Best not to keep him waiting. You know how your father is when he's in a mood."

Kitty hastened down the stairs, followed closely by her mother and Juliet. When she reached the bottom, Beaucroft took her by the arm and practically dragged her into the drawing room. She winced when she saw the vein pulsing at his temple.

"Whatever is the matter, Papa?"

"More scandal and gossip! Did Lord Philip attempt to ravish you in the garden last night?"

Juliet and Mrs. Beaucroft gasped.

"Heavens, no! Who would say such a despicable thing?" Kitty exclaimed.

"Lord Gryphon."

Her blood ran cold. *What a wicked, wicked man!* "It isn't true, Papa. Lord Philip never touched me."

"Furthermore, Lord Groton and Mr. Miller have vouched for his account of events. Why would the three of them invent such a slander?"

Her knees began to shake, and she sank onto a settee. *There is nothing to do now but confess. No matter what the consequences to me, I cannot let Papa believe the worst of Lord Philip.* With a sigh of resignation, Kitty related the story, showing the bruises on her wrists as proof.

"Why didn't you tell me, child?" Beaucroft asked, aghast.

Her lower lip trembled. "I was afraid of the scandal. I've managed everything badly and now both Lord Philip and I are ruined."

A tear traced a path from the inside corner of her eye down her cheek. To Kitty's surprise, her father patted her shoulder and pressed his handkerchief into her hand.

"Don't cry. I deserve most—if not all—of the blame. I shouldn't have pushed you to accept Lord Gryphon. My goal of having you marry well blinded me to his bad character."

Her father's admission took some of the sting away, but nothing could improve the situation except for her departure.

"Thank you for that, Papa. I'll take the train to Grandmama's house in the morning."

"Yes, you must leave London, but you can't go without first clearing Lord Philip of these charges."

"Of course, but how am I to do so?"

The butler appeared. "Excuse me, but Lord Elbourne and Lord Philip have come to call."

"What propitious timing. Please show them in, Watson," Beaucroft said.

As PHILIP and his brother were ushered into the drawing room, he was apprehensive. Miss Beaucroft would certainly exonerate him, but would her father be more inclined to believe his daughter or the rumors? He could see at a glance Miss Beaucroft had been crying and his heart went out to her. Far from being bellicose, Mr. Beaucroft had almost a sheepish expression as he shook Philip's hand.

"Sir, my daughter has confessed everything to me. Lord Gryphon has slandered you in the worst possible manner, and we've just been discussing how best to refute his allegations."

"Thank you. I can assure you, I'm quite grateful for your help." *My faith in Miss Beaucroft was not misplaced; she's forthright and honest where many women would have dissembled.*

"I'll merely tell my side of the story and expose Lord Gryphon as a scurrilous reprobate." Kitty shrugged. "It's as simple as that."

"No, you can't," Philip said. "To admit you were alone with the man will damage your reputation."

"Yours has been sullied far worse!" she exclaimed. "My reputation doesn't matter anymore anyway. As soon as you're exonerated, I'm to leave London."

"Your offer is admirable, Miss Beaucroft, but even if you take Philip's side, it's still the word of two people against three," Augustus said. "People may choose to believe Gryphon."

Kitty looked stricken. "Do you have any other solution to our dilemma, sir?"

"I haven't, I'm afraid."

The wheels began to turn in Philip's head. "I do, but you mightn't like it."

"By all means, sir, please share your thoughts," Beaucroft said.

"We fight a lie with a ruse," Philip said. "We'll invent a plausible story to prove Gryphon and his friends merely *misinterpreted* what they supposedly saw."

"How on earth can we manage that?" Kitty asked.

"We announce our engagement. Gryphon happened upon us just after you accepted my proposal of marriage, you see, and misunderstood our passionate kiss. Since you'd never willingly agree to marry a man who'd attempted to ravish you, Gryphon will come off as a blundering, jealous idiot."

Kitty's blue eyes became wide pools of emotion. "That's a terribly clever ploy, sir, but it's unfair to you. And I can't agree to enter into an engagement in such a manner."

"I understand completely, but I don't mean to suggest an actual engagement. It will secretly be a temporary engagement. Six months from now, society will be talking about some other scandal and we may properly break it off without any harm done to either of us." His gaze slid to Augustus. "Unless you give us away."

"Considering what's at stake, I'll keep your secret."

Kitty glanced at her father. "A ruse seems like our best chance to sidestep a scandal, Papa."

"It's an extremely audacious maneuver!" Mrs. Beaucroft exclaimed. "What will your family say, Lord Philip?"

"Although it pains me to mislead them, I don't plan to tell anyone outside this room that the engagement is temporary. The fewer people who know of the ruse, the better."

"I agree with you, Philip," Augustus said. "Absolute secrecy is paramount. If the truth becomes known, it would be devastating to the reputations of both our families."

Beaucroft nodded. "We are agreed, then. Mrs. Beaucroft and I will officially announce the engagement of our eldest daughter to Lord Philip Butler. Although Lord Gryphon deserves to be set down in the strongest possible terms, we must settle for publicly dismissing his account as a terrible mistake."

Kitty stood and extended her hand to Philip. "Thank you, sir, for coming to my rescue last night. You certainly deserve better thanks than a trumped-up engagement."

He brushed his lips across the back of her hand. "Not at all, Miss Beaucroft. I was honored to be of service in your hour of need."

A warm glow followed her sweet smile.

WHEN PHILIP BROKE the news to his extended family over dinner that night, Eve was confounded.

"Did I hear you correctly? Miss Beaucroft and you are *engaged?*"

"I can scarcely believe it," Trestlebury said.

Despite their somewhat insulting reactions, Philip found he was enjoying the ruse immensely. "I know it's a bit unconventional, but I think we're made for each other."

"It's incredibly romantic." A dreamy expression transformed Prudence's face. "I must tat Miss Beaucroft some lace for her trousseau."

"How did you get her father to agree?" Eve asked.

"When he was presented with the sincerity of our feelings, he could not deny his permission for us to wed," Philip said.

"What an extremely laudable and fair-minded position for Mr. Beaucroft to take," Prudence said. "He must love his daughter very much to put her sentiments over his ambition."

Eve's glance shifted to Augustus. "What say you to all this? I thought you had your eye on the girl."

"A better man got there before me. I wish my brother and Miss Beaucroft every happiness."

Augustus' long-suffering air was a nice touch, in Philip's opinion.

Trestlebury frowned. "Lord Gryphon deserves to be censured for making such a dreadful mistake, and for involving his friends, too! I can only assume his good judgment was clouded by jealousy."

"The only judgment he possesses is bad judgment," Philip said.

"His actions were unforgivable," Augustus said. "Just look at my brother's injuries!"

A wry smile tugged at Philip's swollen lips. "I'll heal, but Gryphon will always be a pompous idiot."

"Well, I *am* surprised," Eve said. "But now that I think about it, Philip and Miss Beaucroft make an absolutely beautiful couple."

"I thought so last night, when they were dancing together," Prudence said. "They caused a bit of a commotion, actually."

"How could you possibly notice?" Trestlebury asked. "Lord Kirkham was monopolizing you."

"He did not monopolize me!"

"Furthermore, when he inserted himself in the brawl, he demonstrated a singular lack of breeding."

"He was coming to Philip's aid!"

"Never mind that now," Eve said. "Prudence and I are attending a ladies' tea tomorrow morning. I don't want to steal Miss Beaucroft's thunder, but considering the rumors about Philip, I hope you don't mind if I reveal this news to our acquaintances?"

"Actually, the sooner everyone knows the facts about what happened, the better," Philip said. "I was reluctant to say anything until the announcement of the engagement appears in the paper, but I'm told Gryphon is spreading lies."

"I don't think we should entertain Lord Gryphon at Trestlebury House in the future," Prudence said. "He has a sly and untrustworthy manner."

"I'll certainly suggest he be dropped socially to everyone who's anyone," Trestlebury said. "Trust me when I say my word carries some weight."

"Lord Groton and Mr. Miller, too," Eve said. "All three should be censured."

Philip was touched by his family's support. "I knew I could count on you."

"Indeed you may. And I should very much like to host your engagement party," Eve said.

Guilt seeped into his consciousness. "Oh, you needn't go to such trouble."

"Well, of course I must!" She beamed. "I do so look forward to knowing Miss Beaucroft better."

"I like her very much," Prudence said. "I think she's quite nice."

"She's very nice indeed," Philip replied.

"I MUST WRITE to Ivy regarding Kitty's engagement," Mrs. Beaucroft said over dinner.

Beaucroft winced. "Do we have to involve my mother?"

"She's part of the family, and Kitty's only surviving grandparent. What if she hears the news from another source?"

"All right, but she'll be on the next train to town." An air of resignation accompanied Beaucroft's assent. "It's not a bad idea, really, now that I think about it. When Mother returns home, Kitty can accompany her."

"Must I?" Kitty's appetite diminished instantly.

"Now that everything's been *managed*, must we send her away?" Mrs. Beaucroft asked.

"Exactly." Kitty perked up, only to deflate again at her father's response.

"Absolutely," Beaucroft said. "She'll stay out of trouble at Mother's house."

"And Kitty won't be subjected to any probing questions in the country," Juliet said.

"Except by Grandmama," Kitty said.

With great effort, she kept a note of dejection from her voice. She would miss the unparalleled bustle and excitement of London, as well as the pageantry and splendor of the Season. But she supposed being cloistered in the country with her reputation intact was better than being banished in disgrace.

The following morning, Kitty received a letter from Lady Trestlebury in which she offered to host an engagement party for her and Philip. As she considered her answer, she was torn. Since the engagement wasn't genuine, could she properly demur without seeming to be ungrateful?

Kitty posed the question to her mother as she was getting dressed to go to the dressmaker's shop with Juliet.

"How do you think I should respond? Considering the circumstances, to accept would be a terrible imposition."

"Why of course you must accept! It would look quite strange otherwise."

"But it's not right! Lady Trestlebury ought not go to the expense and trouble of a party to celebrate a temporary engagement that isn't even genuine."

"Who knows? An actual engagement may come out of this in due course."

"You want me to marry Philip?"

"Certainly not. I'm referring to Lord Elbourne, whose regard for you will no doubt increase upon closer acquaintance."

"Using Philip to secure his brother is despicable behavior by anyone's reckoning."

"Why take that into consideration if you're to be a marchioness one day?"

Her mother's attitude was appalling, but Kitty didn't want to argue the point. Nothing she would say could change her mother's mind.

"May I go with you and Juliet on your outing?" she asked.

"Until the engagement is known, your father thinks it's best for you to keep to the house," Mrs. Beaucroft said. "Why don't you write to your grandmother while we're gone and tell her the news? Afterward, you may answer Lady Trestlebury's letter."

"Yes, Mama."

Long before noon, Augustus and Lord Trestlebury headed off to their respective clubs to refute the ugly gossip regarding Philip and Miss Beaucroft with news of their betrothal. Eve and Prudence went to their ladies' tea with every intention of doing the same. Meanwhile, Philip dashed off a note to his father, informing him and his mother of the engagement. He debated whether to mention Grovebrook in the same letter, but decided against it in the end. There was no need to be overbearing, and his father was certainly intelligent enough to grasp the implications of his pending nuptials.

He sent his valet off to post the letter, and thereafter cast about for something else to do. Being housebound chafed, but Augustus had cautioned him against appearing anywhere in public until the rumors of his alleged indiscretion had been quashed. Although it wasn't strictly proper for him to call on a lady before late afternoon, he decided to call on Miss Beaucroft anyway. After all, they were affianced, even if it was a pretense. No doubt she'd been given the same advice as *he* had—to remain out of view until the engagement was well-known. Her father had mentioned he would be sending an announcement to the newspaper, but there was no telling how quickly it would appear. No matter; whenever gossip was especially juicy, word of mouth was the fastest method of dissemination in society.

Philip donned his hat and set off down the street on foot. That morning, his looking glass had confirmed the swelling in his lips had disappeared. Even though a slight discoloration remained under his eye, he felt far more presentable than he had the day before. As he strode past the luxurious row houses ubiquitous to Belgravia, Philip reflected on what Gryphon's reaction would be when he realized he'd been outfoxed. Certainly, he'd never admit to having fabricated the entire story out of whole cloth. The lout would be forced to save face by apologizing for his grievous mistake. The thought made Philip chuckle, startling an elderly woman out for a walk with her poodle.

At the Beaucroft residence, the butler showed him into the drawing room. Kitty joined him shortly thereafter.

"Oh, hello! I'm so glad you've come. I just finished writing a letter to your cousin, Lady Trestlebury. Perhaps you would be good enough to deliver it for me?"

"I'd be delighted."

She studied his face. "You're looking ever so much better, albeit still a little colorful."

"That I am. Say, it's rather nice out. Would you fancy a stroll?"

Her eyes widened. "Without a chaperone?"

"No chaperone necessary if we're engaged."

"I hadn't thought of that! How very jolly."

Her laugh was conspiratorial and he joined in.

"Let me fetch my hat and we'll be off," she said.

A few minutes later, they left the house together. Kitty took his arm, and they walked toward the park.

"Did you know Lady Trestlebury offered to host an engagement party for us? I feel a little guilty about accepting, but it can't be helped if we're to maintain our ruse."

"I also feel some regret about misleading my relations. But as you say, it can't be helped."

"Speaking of dissembling, I sent off a letter to my grandmother before you arrived. She'll likely come to town as soon as she receives it. She's rather fierce, I warn you."

"Perhaps I can win her over."

"Maybe so, but you won't have a great deal of time. Despite our engagement, my father has decided I'm to go live with her after all. We'll probably leave after the engagement party."

"How long will you be away?"

"Until I toss you aside, I think. Sooner, perhaps, if Juliet becomes engaged."

"An eternity to be separated from the delights of town."

"Yes, but society will have forgotten my scandals when I return…only to cast me in the role of villain for jilting you." The last part was delivered in a teasing manner.

"I could jilt you, if you'd prefer."

"No, I must jilt you! It will lend you an air of tragedy and attract all manner of ladies to comfort you in your melancholy."

"Aha! If I weren't determined to stay a bachelor that would be exactly what I need."

"May I call you Philip?"

"Of course."

"Please call me Kitty."

"Thank you. I hope we can be friends, despite this silly situation. Our ordeal will be much more bearable that way, don't you think?"

"I'd like that, but I'm not sure I'd call it an ordeal. Maybe more of an intrigue."

He laughed. "That's far more exciting, definitely."

"Tell me why you wish to remain a bachelor?"

"I'm ineligible. If I can't court any woman I choose without making an apology for my circumstances, I'll court none."

"Seems a harsh business, but I think I understand."

They found a bench in the shade, and sat talking for over an hour. Finally, she wrinkled her pert nose. "Am I boring you with my girlish prattling?"

"Not at all. Besides which, as your fiancé, I might be expected to know a little about you."

"So you might."

He gave her a rueful glance and stood. "As much as I've enjoyed our conversation, I mustn't run afoul of my future mother-in-law by keeping you out too long."

They returned the way they had come, and he waited in the entryway while Kitty went upstairs to fetch her letter to Eve. He slipped the envelope in his coat pocket and promised faithfully to deliver it.

"Thank you for the outing," he said. "Let's do it again."

"Yes, let's. After all, the engagement announcement should be published soon, and we must be seen in public together."

"I've been invited to Lady Lovejoy's ball this Wednesday night," Philip said. "I was going to beg off, but if you would accompany me, I can be persuaded to change my mind."

"I'd be pleased to attend the ball with you. We were planning to go anyway, but I'd much rather go with you than with my parents."

"I'll pick you up in the carriage at eight. And would you like to go riding Wednesday morning, before breakfast?"

"I'd adore it!" She laughed. "This playacting is going to be so much fun, Philip! During our temporary engagement, I'll be able to flirt with you to my heart's content! You won't take it seriously, will you?"

"I wouldn't dare. And I'll practice wooing you as ardently as possible, as long as you aren't offended."

"I wouldn't dare."

He gave her a smoldering glance as he straightened from kissing her hand. "I'll see you Wednesday morning, then."

"Ooh, that was good. The way you looked at me just now made a little shiver go down my spine."

"Really? Then it stays in my repertoire."

Humming under his breath, Philip left the Beaucroft residence and set off for Trestlebury House. His footsteps slowed when it suddenly occurred to him that a girl like Kitty deserved a ring of engagement. A family heirloom would be made available to Augustus to present to *his* intended, but Philip had no such bauble at his disposal. He hailed an approaching cab.

"I'm in the market for an engagement ring," he said to the cab driver.

The man touched his hat. "I know just the place, Guv'nor. Climb aboard."

AUGUSTUS AND BEAUCROFT met at their Pall Mall gentlemen's club, to present a united front in their quest to clear Philip's name. Augustus kept one eye out for Lord Gryphon, and at length the man strode in as if he possessed the establishment. Ordinarily, Augustus viewed himself as imperturbable, but he felt a surge of antipathy at Gryphon's presence.

He blocked his path. "Excuse me, sir, but I believe you owe my brother an apology."

Gryphon laughed. "I can't imagine why, unless he feels the thrashing he received was insufficient to teach him a lesson."

Beaucroft joined Augustus. "You mistook the situation entirely. I'd given Lord Philip permission to speak to my daughter, you see. She'd just agreed to become his wife when you happened upon them."

Gryphon's eyes narrowed. "That's the most ridiculous thing I've ever heard. It didn't happen that way, and you know it."

"Indeed, I do not," Beaucroft said. "My daughter is engaged to Lord Philip, and you've slandered an innocent man."

"In fact, unless you withdraw your accusations and apologize, I'll be forced to seek legal counsel on my brother's behalf," Augustus said. "Since we're all gentlemen, such recourse shouldn't be necessary."

Several members of the club had clustered around the trio as the confrontation unfolded. After Augustus made his demands, voices rang out, urging Gryphon to apologize. His face deepened in color, as if his head would explode, and a muscle in his jaw quivered. Augustus kept an impassive expression as he watched a myriad of emotions flit across the man's visage. *He's cornered, and he knows it.*

Finally, Gryphon gave a curt nod. "My concern for Miss Beaucroft's welfare was uppermost on my mind. If I mistook the situation, I apologize. I wish Lord Philip a speedy recovery, and every happiness with his engagement."

The surrounding gentlemen breathed a collective sigh of relief. Neither Beaucroft nor Augustus moved to shake Gryphon's hand, and he made no effort to shake theirs. Instead, he collected his hat and left the club. His posture was ramrod straight, and he was quivering with suppressed rage.

When Augustus and Beaucroft were alone, they exchanged an amused glance.

"Shall we dine?" Augustus suggested.

"Yes, indeed," Beaucroft replied. "After such a satisfying experience, I believe I've worked up a tremendous appetite."

THE ROMANCE

When Mrs. Beaucroft and Juliet returned from the dressmaker, Kitty told them about Philip's visit. Her mother gave her a horrified look. "You went for a walk with Lord Philip, *unchaperoned?*"

Kitty bit back a laugh. Her mother made it sound as though she'd skipped through the East End with her skirts hiked up over her ankles.

"Why of course, Mama. We're engaged."

"In name only! Furthermore, the announcement has not yet appeared in the paper. What if someone we know saw you?"

"Their curiosity will soon be satisfied when they learn Philip and I are engaged."

Her mother's lips tightened. "I forbid you from seeing the man."

"You can scarcely do that when we wish to convince the world the engagement is genuine, Mama," Juliet said. "Besides which, what harm can it do? Kitty will be leaving London after Lady Trestlebury's engagement party, and she'll probably not see Philip for a long time—if ever."

Kitty gave her sister a smile of gratitude for her support. "Quite so."

"Well, I suppose if you put it that way, I must concede the point," Mrs. Beaucroft said. "But keep contact with Lord Philip to a bare minimum, and only when it's strictly necessary. We should encourage Lord Elbourne's interest, not give him the impression you're becoming overly attached to his brother."

"Philip is escorting me to Lady Lovejoy's ball."

"*What?*"

"We must attempt to act affianced, Mama, if only for a little while."

Mrs. Beaucroft threw her hands up in the air. "I give up!"

Juliet edged toward the stairs. "Come see my new gown, Kitty."

The two sisters closeted themselves in Juliet's room, ignoring the new gown hanging on a wall hook.

"What was it like to walk with Lord Philip without Bridget or Mama tagging along?" Juliet asked.

"I've never felt more relaxed and free in my life. Philip and I talked half the morning, and I feel it wasn't long enough. Being engaged is absolutely heavenly."

"I'm so envious! You're able to go to Lady Lovejoy's ball with an escort and I must attend with Mama and Papa." Juliet pouted.

"Don't tell Mama, but Philip and I are going riding Wednesday morning. I'll be home before breakfast."

Juliet gave her a sidelong glance. "You're fond of him, aren't you?"

"We're good friends, nothing more."

"I should tell you…according to Violet, Lord Philip was quite smitten with her last year."

Kitty was not inclined to listen to anything Miss Haver had to say about anything. "Such gossip can be of no consequence to me."

When Kitty joined her family in the drawing room before dinner that evening, she was pleased to discover her father had returned from his club in a rare good humor.

"I gather from your expression that Lord Gryphon's slander has been successfully addressed?"

"Indeed it has, and it gave me untold pleasure to set that rascal down. Lord Elbourne and I worked Lord Gryphon over thoroughly, and he was forced to apologize in front of dozens of our acquaintances. He left the club in a fit of apoplexy, but I believe Lord Philip's reputation has been redeemed. Furthermore, your engagement is the talk of London."

Kitty threw her arms around him. "Oh, thank you, Papa!"

He chuckled. "You're quite welcome. Lord Elbourne is a very steady fellow, and I should like to see you properly wed to him, when the time comes."

Her smile slipped only a little. "Yes, sir."

The butler appeared with a small box and envelope on a silver salver and presented it to Kitty. "This was just delivered for you, miss."

"Thank you, Watson," Beaucroft said.

"A gift from you, Papa?" Kitty asked.

"Why, no." Beaucroft seemed genuinely puzzled.

She opened the envelope. "It's from Philip!"

Juliet hastened over to watch her open the box. Inside was a gold Claddagh ring with two deep red stones forming the heart in the center.

"Are those garnets?" Juliet asked. "Garnets are Her Majesty's favorite stones!"

As Kitty slid the beautiful ring onto her finger, she felt tears sting her eyelids. The traditional Irish symbol, with its hands of friendship, the crown for loyalty, and the heart for affection, seemed to embody her relationship with Philip in every regard.

"It's perfect."

Mrs. Beaucroft examined the ring with a critical eye. "The lad has good taste in jewelry, I'll grant you. No doubt his brother advised him."

"Well, then, all the trappings of an engagement are complete." Beaucroft nodded. "After your engagement party, we may put this hideous nightmare behind us."

PHILIP'S RIDE on Rotten Row with Kitty Wednesday morning wasn't vigorous exercise, but he enjoyed it nonetheless. The engagement announcement had appeared in the paper the day before, and it seemed everyone who was anyone was out riding and had heard the news. They were obliged to rein in their horses every few yards or so, to chat with well-wishers and friends.

Philip found himself the recipient of many appraising glances, and he hoped the last yellowed vestiges of his bruise gave him a devil-may-care appearance. Kitty's engagement ring was much admired, and he inwardly thanked the jeweler who'd provided it. A lesser gold band would have sufficed, but from the way Kitty's eyes had sparkled when she thanked him earlier made him glad he'd gone to the trouble and expense.

When he returned to Trestlebury House for breakfast, Philip was surprised to discover his parents had come to town on the morning train. Lord and Lady Trestlebury, Prudence, Augustus, and Lord and Lady Moregate were assembled in the dining room.

"Well, hullo. I'm not sure I expected to see you quite so soon," Philip said.

As he gave his mother a kiss on the cheek, she frowned at the sight of his battered face. "You've been getting into trouble again."

"Er...it's a long story." Philip slid onto a chair.

"It always is."

"You're looking uncommonly well, Mother."

Lady Moregate snorted. "Flattery will not dissuade me from the task at hand. Your father and I came as soon as we could. We wish to talk some sense into you."

A smile played on Augustus' lips, but Eve, Trestlebury, and Prudence immediately fixed their attention on their plates.

Philip gave his mother and father bewildered glances. "In what way?"

Moregate almost glowered at him. "We're determined to dissuade you from this course of action!"

"Your father sent you to get a *suitable* bride, not the most famous beauty in all London!" Lady Moregate exclaimed. "Are you sure Miss Beaucroft knows you're the *second* son?"

"I told her almost straightaway."

She shook her head in disapproval. "Be under no illusion, your father won't increase your allowance just because you're marrying a girl like her. Don't you realize Miss Beaucroft won't be satisfied with your income? Your marriage is bound to be a disaster!"

Although Philip understood his parents' concerns were for naught, their objections rankled. He'd resisted matrimony for just the reasons they'd stated and had made no secret of it. Now that he'd supposedly acquiesced to their demands, his parents seemed to be rubbing his nose in his lack of status. Despite his anger, he bit back a sharp retort. He still needed his father to sell Grovebrook to him and being disagreeable wouldn't help matters whatsoever.

"Kitty and I don't intend to rush into matrimony, I can assure you. I have much to do as far as Grovebrook is concerned, and she's in no hurry. We've plenty of time to contemplate what sort of future lies ahead of us as a couple, and I wouldn't dream of asking you for an increase in my allowance. In fact, I'd far rather live on the income from Grovebrook."

"What's all this about Grovebrook?" Trestlebury asked.

"An idea has lodged in Philip's mind and he won't let it go," Moregate said. "He's asked me to sell him a poorly performing property in the country, consisting of a small town and a handful of farms. He believes he can turn it around."

"I expect he can," Augustus said. "Philip usually accomplishes anything he sets his mind to. He was first in his class at Oxford."

Philip was grateful for his brother's loyalty. "Thank you for that, Augustus. I want to own land, and I'm willing to work for it."

"It's a lofty and worthy goal," Prudence said. "And why shouldn't a man of modest means be just as entitled to love and happiness as a rich one?"

Trestlebury rolled his eyes. "How very democratic."

"Please, Daniel." Eve turned her attention to Philip. "Grovebrook is a backwater hamlet, isn't it? You may have quite a challenge on your hands to make it a success."

"Oh, I don't know," Philip replied. "It's well-situated midway between Leeds and Lancaster, and there's a train station to serve our needs not two miles from the center of town."

"Have you been there recently?" Eve asked.

"Not since I was a child, but I was completely charmed by the town and its people back then and have never forgotten it," Philip said. "The manor house has been uninhabited for quite some time, so it will need a bit of sprucing up to make it livable, I'm sure."

"A great deal of work for little return, if you ask me," Lady Moregate said. "And since Miss Beaucroft will quite certainly dislike living in the country year 'round, the endeavor will provide yet another reason for the marriage to founder."

To avoid making a heated retort, Philip buttered a fruited muffin and took a large bite.

"Truly, Mother, you are worried for no reason," Augustus said. "When you meet Miss Beaucroft, her good-humor and sweet nature will win you over. And, as Philip said, the engagement is to be a lengthy one. Let's see how this all plays out."

"I have my doubts about Grovebrook *and* your choice of bride, Philip, but I'm a man of my word," Moregate said. "Since you've done what I asked and Augustus has endorsed the enterprise, I'll have my attorney draft up the contract for purchase."

Philip's ill humor evaporated, and a broad grin burst forth. "That's simply marvelous."

KITTY WAS BUOYANT. Her ride on Rotten Row had caused a rather satisfying commotion, and Philip had cut a fine figure on his beautiful steed. The steady stream of callers at home mid-morning pleased her as well. Since Mrs. Beaucroft was cloistered with the housekeeper, arranging menus for the upcoming month, Kitty and Juliet received callers, all intimate friends, by themselves in the drawing room.

Everyone was curious about Lord Philip Butler, naturally, and Kitty entertained them with a myriad of interesting details she'd learned only recently. Few girls departed without making a disparaging comment or two about Lord Gryphon. All agreed that his jealousy had led to the egregious assault on Philip and was unattractive in the extreme. As for Kitty, she was as congenial and magnanimous as possible by expressing her pity for Gryphon and wondering delicately if he ought not consider a lengthy trip abroad to settle his nerves.

"You're certainly enjoying yourself," Juliet said after the last visitor left.

"Tremendously."

"But you're always the center of attention. Doesn't it become a little tiresome?"

Kitty gave a satisfied sigh. "I'm soaking it up for when I'm in exile."

"Surely you won't fail to find admirers in the country, too."

Kitty was taken aback at her sister's flat tone. "You must think me terribly shallow."

Juliet's smile seemed forced. "Of course not." Another arrival rang the doorbell just then, and she made an exasperated noise. "The Queen herself doesn't have this many callers in one day!"

An imposing older woman strode into the drawing room a few moments later, without waiting for the butler to announce her.

Kitty jumped to her feet. "Grandmama!"

Mrs. Ivy Beaucroft's lips were compressed together and her eyes flashed. "Juliet, please go find your mother and tell her I've arrived. I'd like to have a word with Kitty alone."

"Yes, Grandmama."

As her grandmother removed her coat and hat, Juliet hastened from the room.

"Er...you must have received my letter? I'm so glad you've come," Kitty said.

"No you're not. Undoubtedly, I'm the last person you wish to see. Now what's all this nonsense about marrying Lord Philip Butler? I could scarcely believe my eyes when I read your news."

"He's perfectly charming, Grandmama, and—"

"I don't care if he's the Pied Piper of Hamelin! Your family expects you to marry a duke, marquess, earl, or at the very least an exceedingly wealthy viscount. Lord Philip may have many fine qualities, but the only way he'll inherit his father's title is if his elder brother dies without having a son. And since Lord Elbourne is exceedingly youthful and healthy by all reports, that possibility is slim indeed. What am I not being told? Is there a scandal of which I should be made aware?"

"N-No."

"You're lying to me, Constance. I can always tell when you're not being absolutely truthful." Her voice lowered to a whisper. "Are you in a *delicate* condition?"

"Grandmama!" Kitty felt the blush clear up to the roots of her hair. "Since you insist on thinking the worst of me, I must tell you everything."

After she related how she came to be engaged, Ivy finally took a deep breath and smiled. "I'm so relieved."

Mrs. Beaucroft and Juliet hastened into the room.

"Ivy, are you unwell?" Mrs. Beaucroft exclaimed.

"I had a turn for a moment, but Kitty has set my mind at ease by confessing the truth about this ridiculous betrothal."

"Now you must promise me faithfully to play along as if the engagement is real," Kitty said.

The older woman beamed. "Oh, yes, I can do that. It wouldn't be the first time in this family I've pretended to be happy about an engagement."

Kitty and Juliet exchanged a surreptitious, amused glance. Their father was Ivy's only child, so there was only one engagement to which she could be referring. Mrs. Beaucroft, who had apparently caught Ivy's meaning full well, narrowed her eyes. "I'll have the maids make up your room and set another place for lunch."

"My son is at his club, I imagine? Good, it'll be just us ladies."

"I hope you brought some evening gowns, Ivy." Mrs. Beaucroft's voice was icily polite. "We're to attend Lady Lovejoy's ball tonight."

"I believe my maid packed all manner of gowns, but I wouldn't dream of attending the ball. I can't abide uninvited guests, and I'm certain Lady Lovejoy feels the same." Ivy turned her attention to Juliet. "How have you been enjoying London, dear?"

"For the most part, it's been wonderful. I mean, I was horribly nervous at court when I was presented to Her Majesty. But everyone has been lovely, and I've had a marvelous time."

"She led off the dancing at the Trestlebury ball," Kitty said. "Juliet has been much admired."

"I'm so happy to hear it. It's always difficult being a younger sister, and even more so when the elder sister is a famous beauty. People always have the unfortunate tendency to compare."

THE CARRIAGE RIDE to Lady Lovejoy's mansion wasn't overly long, so Kitty savored every moment she had alone with Philip. She'd asked Juliet if she wanted to come along, but her sister had demurred. Since her sister had been slightly out of sorts of late, Kitty was secretly relieved.

"Do you know, this is my first time alone in a carriage with a man who isn't a relative," she said. "Mama is fit to be tied about it, but there's nothing she can do. I daresay she's in the carriage behind us, urging the driver to go faster."

"She doesn't like me?"

"Please don't be offended. It's nothing personal."

His smile was sardonic. "I understand completely. I'm unsuitable for a girl like you."

Her eyes widened. "I'm sorry, Philip. I didn't mean—"

"Don't give it another thought. My parents told me precisely the same thing when they tried to persuade me to break things off. You'll meet them at the ball tonight. They came to town on the morning train."

A moment of panic. "If I'd known I was to meet your parents, I would have worn a more modest gown!"

A chuckle. "Perish the thought. You're perfect just as you are, and I'm quite looking forward to the view."

Although she flushed with pleasure at his comment, Kitty tapped his knee with her fan as punishment. "Naughty lad. As it turns out, my grandmother came to town today as well."

"Came to register her objections, did she?"

"I'm afraid so. Grandmama is a trifle difficult to please. Fortunately, she won't be at the ball tonight."

"I can breathe a little easier, then."

Heads turned and tongues wagged when they entered Lady Lovejoy's home a short time later. Kitty handed off her cape to a servant and turned toward Philip to take his arm. His gaze glided over her face and figure with admiration, and for once she reveled in the display of her décolletage.

"You really are blindingly beautiful this evening," he said. "Am I allowed to say so?"

"I would be devastated if you didn't."

In the receiving line, Kitty introduced Philip to Lady Lovejoy, a widowed matron with sharp eyes and a strong jaw.

"Lord Philip, your cousin Eve is a dear friend of mine." She smiled at Kitty. "I shall count upon receiving an invitation to your wedding."

Kitty gulped. Lady Lovejoy was in the very upper echelons of society, and to have her attend one's wedding was a major triumph.

"W-Why, thank you," she managed.

As she and Philip made their way into the ballroom, Kitty gave his arm an excited squeeze. "What an honor!"

His quizzical glance reminded her there was to be no wedding.

"I'm sorry. I've been so caught up in our ruse, I'm forgetting it's a game," she said.

"It's all right if you're enjoying it. I'm enjoying it, too."

"It occurs to me there shall eventually be negative consequences to our present course of action. Your cousins and Lady Lovejoy will resent me for throwing you over."

"I won't let them say a word against you. The more I think about it, I should be the jilt."

"I couldn't let you do that."

"You can and you shall."

"Oh, Philip, you're so wonderful. Lean down so I can kiss your cheek…quickly while no one is looking."

She deposited the kiss.

"You're such a flirt," he teased.

A giggle. "I had planned to introduce you to your next fiancée, but I'm not sure any of my acquaintances are good enough for you."

"Remember, I'm not inclined to marry at all."

"We can't have that."

"Once I've made my fortune, I daresay I'll be an infinitely better catch. If I marry, it will be to a woman who is proud to call herself my wife, not one who wishes she could have done better."

"Philip, not every girl is like Miss Haver."

He flinched. "How do you know about her?"

"She mentioned something about you to Juliet."

"Lovely."

Gryphon's snide, familiar voice interrupted their conversation. "Well, if it isn't the happy couple."

He'd paused a few feet away, with Violet Haver on his arm. The sour look on Gryphon's face made it appear he'd eaten something unpleasant off one of the trays of appetizers being passed around by the servants. Violet, on the other hand, was simpering at Gryphon in a sticky sweet and clearly besotted fashion. Kitty had to force herself not to physically recoil.

"Zachary and I may soon be announcing our own engagement," Miss Haver said.

Gryphon frowned. "Violet, I daresay you've overshot the mark."

"I think you should follow through, Gryphon," Philip said. "I've rarely seen two people more suited to one another than you and Miss Haver."

He steered Kitty away.

"That was a perfectly dreadful thing for you to say," she whispered.

"You disagree?"

"You misunderstand me. I meant it as a compliment."

THE LOOK of irritation on Lord Gryphon's face alarmed Violet. "I'm sorry if I spoke out of turn," she said. "I just assumed you wouldn't mind."

"You were wrong."

They watched Kitty and Philip circulate through the crowd, greeting friends and responding to congratulations in an ebullient manner.

"They're making an absolute spectacle of themselves," Violet said. "Furthermore, Miss Beaucroft's gown would be better suited to a tart. I can't believe she's lowering herself to marry someone as poor as Lord Philip Butler."

"Don't be ridiculous. No marriage will ever take place, I can assure you. They've come together temporarily only to save their respective reputations."

"What?"

"I've no proof just yet, but the notion she'd agree to marry a man of no consequence defies common sense."

"Perhaps she's attracted to him. He *is* handsome."

Gryphon's cool glance prompted a correction.

"But not nearly as handsome as you are."

"You're friendly with Miss Beaucroft's sister. If you wish to prove your devotion to me, you'll obtain confirmation from Miss Juliet that her sister's arrangement with Butler is a ruse."

"What do you intend to do with the information?"

"Expose them, of course. Butler and Miss Beaucroft may think they've made a fool of me, but they won't get away with it."

"You understand you'll be responsible for besmirching their families, don't you?"

"You care more about them than you do for me?"

"Why no, but I'm rather fond of Juliet."

She focused on her friend, who was studying her dance card several yards off. Gryphon followed her gaze.

"There she is now. If you wish to marry me, don't return until you've managed it."

He was deadly serious, and she realized she had no choice. None at all.

"I'll manage it."

A welcoming smile accompanied Violet as she glided across the floor. "I'm so glad you've arrived, Juliet!"

She bestowed air kisses on both of Juliet's cheeks.

"Hello, Violet. You're absolutely glowing!"

"You're too kind. Your gown is simply splendid, and I'm not sure you've ever looked better."

"Thank you! For once I managed to arrive at a ball without creasing my skirt. Lord Philip brought Kitty here in a separate carriage, you see, so I had a whole seat to myself."

"Much excitement has happened lately, hasn't it?"

"Indeed, events were altogether too exciting for a time, but it has worked out for the best."

"For others, perhaps, but I'm not so sure it's worked out well for *you*."

"What do you mean?"

"Your first Season has been ruined by your sister!"

"Ruined?" Juliet frowned. "That's an exaggeration, don't you agree?"

"Not in the least! Her engagement is all anyone will talk of for months, and it's unfair. Really, Juliet, you're a saint. You're constantly being overshadowed, and I can't see how you put up with her."

"It *is* hard sometimes, but I don't believe Kitty means to outshine me on purpose."

Violet made a sound of disgust. "I have no trouble believing it whatsoever. At any rate, we've got to find a way to turn things around for you, or you'll be pushed to the back of the bin."

"Kitty is quitting London in a few weeks. When she's gone, my social schedule will no longer be disrupted."

"Come with me. I must tell you something in confidence." Violet tugged Juliet by the hand until they reached a private corner. "Lord Gryphon maintains it was your sister who lured him out to the garden. She begged him to propose to her, and when he refused, she struck him. That's when Lord Philip stumbled onto the situation and misinterpreted everything."

Juliet appeared to be nonplussed. "But originally, Lord Gryphon claimed to have seen Lord Philip take liberties. Why would he invent such a story?"

"To protect your sister's reputation, of course! She already has a reputation for being a flirt. If everyone knew she'd thrown herself at Lord Gryphon, she would have been undone."

"My sister wouldn't lie to me about it, Violet. I saw the bruises on her wrists."

"Bruises she sustained when Lord Gryphon tried to prevent her from striking him again."

"That's silly."

"I'm just relating what I heard." Violet projected innocence. "Between you and me, I believe Lord Philip is a fortune hunter."

"You characterize the man unfairly."

"Lord Gryphon knows him from Oxford and says he talked constantly of marrying an heiress someday."

"That's not so!"

"Lord Moregate gives Lord Philip only a meager allowance, and the real reason he wants to marry your sister is for her dowry."

"That can't be true because he's not going to marry her at all!" Juliet bit her lip.

Violet cocked her head. "The engagement has been broken off?"

"No, Kitty and Lord Philip are still engaged. Er...what I meant to say is that he's not going to marry her right away."

"Aha...I think I understand now. To silence the scandal with Lord Gryphon, they agreed to become engaged for a short while with no intention of actually marrying. My goodness, what a calculated ploy!"

"I didn't say that!"

"You don't have to, Juliet. I understand your loyalty to your sister, but if people knew the truth, they'd be livid. Nobody likes to be played for a fool."

"You've misunderstood me! I misspoke myself because you were maligning Lord Philip's character. He's a very decent, honorable gentleman."

A smile. "I'm sure he makes a wonderful imaginary future brother-in-law."

"Don't tease, Violet. You must promise not to repeat that ridiculous story to anyone."

"Don't worry, your secret is safe." She stifled a giggle. "Oh, there's Lady Lovejoy! If you'll excuse me, I must go thank her once again for inviting me."

INTRIGUES AND MACHINATIONS

After his parents arrived at the ball, Philip escorted Kitty over to introduce her.

"This must be the famous Miss Beaucroft," Moregate said. "The reports of your beauty have not been exaggerated."

"And yet she is even more beautiful inside than out," Philip said.

"Thank you both! The gentlemen in the Butler family are indeed generous with their compliments," Kitty said.

Philip turned his attention to his mother. "Kitty, allow me to introduce my mother, Lady Moregate."

The two women curtsied to one another.

"It's an honor to meet you," Kitty said.

"I'm curious, after such a short acquaintance, why you've agreed to marry my youngest son," Lady Moregate said.

"Mother," Philip said, warningly.

"It's all right, Philip," Kitty said. "Lady Moregate, from the moment I met him, Philip has continued to demonstrate the kindest and most gentlemanly behavior I've ever witnessed. He's truly a gem, and I'm grateful he feels even the slightest esteem for me."

Philip fought to keep his countenance. The praise was so effusive, he was certain his mother would see right through it. Lady Moregate seemed taken aback, however, and responded with a smile.

"He *is* kind, and admittedly the more handsome of my two sons. Still, I caution you to think long and hard about marriage to Philip. Strong unions have been torn asunder by lack of luxury."

Kitty turned her blue eyes toward Philip. "I have faith in him, Lady Moregate."

If he hadn't known better, he would have almost believed her assertion. *Remember, this is just a game. I've promised not to take her seriously.*

"The dancing is about to begin," he said. "Kitty, would you care to dance?"

"Oh, no," Moregate said. "The first dance belongs to me, if Miss Beaucroft will consent to be my partner."

"With pleasure, sir."

Moregate led Kitty toward the dance floor. Lady Moregate laughed and patted Philip's arm. "Don't worry, dear, he won't run away with her."

"What?"

"You looked like a lost puppy just now, when Miss Beaucroft left your side."

"Did I?" He cleared his throat. "Is Augustus here?"

"He's chatting with Lady Lovejoy, but don't change the subject. I see you're completely smitten by your fiancée."

"We're engaged, after all."

"Yes, but many people become engaged who share no affection whatsoever, Philip. Love in marriage is both a blessing and a curse. When you care for someone as deeply as you care for Miss Beaucroft, she has the power to hurt you. Be forewarned."

"Yes, mother. And on that cheerful note, would you like to dance?"

"I would, thank you."

Philip and his mother joined the couples on the dance floor, but he was preoccupied. His mother was wrong; he couldn't be in love with Kitty. To have allowed himself to fall in love with her would be the utmost foolishness, and he wasn't given to foolishness. He was merely pretending to be a love-struck swain, and undoubtedly his expression reflected his role. In addition, Kitty's ability to playact was extremely convincing. *It's a ruse, not a romance, and I mustn't ever forget the difference.*

LORD MOREGATE WAS A PRACTICED and assured dance partner, which came as a relief to Kitty. Ordinarily, she was an excellent dancer, but she was utterly distracted by Philip's comment about her inner beauty. In her experience, most men were exclusively focused on her looks, without regard to her other qualities, so his sentiment had come as a refreshing surprise. Although she realized Philip was merely practicing his courtship technique, she was finding him increasingly irresistible. Her possible feelings for him were a disturbing and unwelcome development. If she should marry Lord Elbourne, would she always secretly yearn for his brother? And when Philip took a bride, would she be forced to feign happiness while hiding her own torment?

Philip came into view as he danced with Lady Moregate. Kitty caught his eye, and his resulting smile made her knees grow weak. *What a horrible joke if I'm in love with a man who is indifferent to me. Please, let it not be true!* Obviously, the game she and Philip were playing had become a dangerous one—for her heart.

Her partner chuckled as he followed her gaze. "I was prepared to disapprove of your marrying my son, but I see my opinion will do no good. I'm not too old to recognize a woman in love."

Kitty's dance steps faltered, but Moregate took it in stride.

"Sorry, I didn't mean to embarrass you," he said. "Your genuine sentiment is refreshing, especially when we're surrounded by some of the most jaded and vainglorious people in England. I find it inspirational."

"Thank you, sir." *Oh, no!*

It WAS a fine afternoon to transact business, and Philip arrived at the attorney's office, near bursting with anticipation and excitement. A week had passed since his father agreed to sell him Grovebrook, and he couldn't wait to sign the papers to make the property his. To the obvious annoyance of the attorney's clerk, who kept clearing his throat in protest, Philip paced in the anteroom while he was waiting to be called in. When at last he was admitted to Mr. Motto's office, a small stack of papers—presumably the contract—sat on the attorney's desk.

"So, young man, I understand congratulations are in order," Mr. Motto said.

"Yes, I've been anticipating this day for quite some time."

The attorney frowned in puzzlement. "I was referring to your engagement to Miss Beaucroft."

"Oh! Yes, that's indeed a stroke of good luck, thank you. I will endeavor to deserve her."

Mr. Motto gestured toward a chair. "Have a seat, milord. Your father has asked me to draw up the papers to Grovebrook in a specific manner. After you read all the provisions, you may ask me any questions that occur to you."

Although he was tempted to skim the contract, Philip forced himself to concentrate and read it line by line. After the preamble, however, it didn't take him long to peer up at the attorney, aghast.

"The sale of Grovebrook is wholly contingent upon the wedding to Miss Beaucroft? This isn't what Father and I discussed at all!"

A nod. "Lord Moregate knew you would be taken aback at the condition, but he felt it was critical you acquire a bride before you take full possession of the property."

"So my signature on this contract means nothing."

"Not at all. Your signature forms a binding contract. However, your rights to Grovebrook won't become perfected until the moment you are wed." The man pursed his lips. "I can assure you, upon this point your father will not be moved."

Philip sat back, stunned. "That's just…brilliant."

Eve, Prudence, and Lady Moregate spent the day shopping, flitting from one shop to another in search of various accessories and shoes.

"I come to town so infrequently, I see very little I don't want to buy," Lady Moregate said. "Fortunately, I have a very understanding husband."

"I wish Papa were half so understanding." Prudence delivered her sentiment in a wistful fashion. "When he forms an opinion, he will not be moved."

They strolled along the pavement, pausing occasionally to admire a store window display. An imposing woman approached from the opposite direction.

"Oh, good morning, Lady Lovejoy!" Eve exclaimed.

"How delightful to see you again," Lady Moregate said.

"Good morning." Although Lady Lovejoy nodded, her tone was frosty.

"Look for an invitation to my cousin's engagement party,"

Eve said. "Philip mentioned you'd asked to be invited to the wedding, and I thought—"

"Forgive me, but my time is too valuable to waste on intrigues and machinations."

Eve was taken aback. "I'm sorry, but I don't catch your meaning."

"I think you know perfectly well what I mean. I've been informed that the betrothal between Miss Beaucroft and Lord Philip Butler is simply a scheme to deflect attention away from their respective scandals. Really, I would have thought you were above contributing to such deceit. Good day to you."

She hastened past. Stunned, Lady Moregate, Eve, and Prudence stared at the woman's retreating back.

"How completely...odd," Eve managed. "Why would Lady Lovejoy say such a horrible thing?"

"What she said can't possibly be true," Lady Moregate murmured, wide eyed. "Somebody has been telling tales at our expense."

"I can't imagine how an ugly rumor like that got started," Prudence said.

"Neither do I...although to be honest, I always felt the engagement was rather unexpected and rushed," Eve said. "Perhaps the timing was too sudden to seem genuine."

"Did she say something about scandals? Nobody mentioned anything about scandals to me." Lady Moregate looked askance at Eve and Prudence. "Perhaps one of you would be kind enough to fill me in."

AFTER AN EXCITING CRICKET match at Lord's, Augustus and Beaucroft waited in a queue for their carriage to be brought around. A well-dressed gentleman approached and hailed Beaucroft.

"Well hullo there! Just the man I wished to see."

"Hullo, Lord Ferndale!"

Beaucroft introduced his friend to Augustus.

"A pleasure to make your acquaintance, sir. Now that I have the two of you together, I must ask you to quash a rather disturbing rumor," Ferndale said. "Is it true Miss Beaucroft's betrothal to Lord Philip Butler is a contrivance?"

"What?" Augustus forced his countenance to remain placid, lifting only one eyebrow to express incredulity at such a ridiculous assertion.

"What a strange notion!" Beaucroft said. "I can assure you, my daughter is planning her wedding even now." A vein in his temple pulsed as he spoke.

Ferndale shook his head, bewildered. "Then it's a terrible falsehood. These gossips ought to be ashamed of themselves."

"Yes. People like to hear themselves talk, I think," Augustus said.

"Well, you should know the story is circulating," Ferndale said. "Perhaps you might want to nudge the wedding plans along, eh?"

He touched the brim of his top hat before ambling off. All conversation between Augustus and Beaucroft was suspended until they'd climbed into their carriage and left the cricket grounds behind.

"How on earth did the truth get out?" Beaucroft muttered finally.

"It's a puzzlement, but I suspect Lord Gryphon is behind this campaign of revenge."

"Kitty saw something in that accursed man's character that gave her pause, but I wouldn't listen. Well, we refuted the story to Ferndale, and undoubtedly the rumor will die quickly."

Augustus tried to brush off the incident, but truthfully he was unsettled.

"I hope you're right. If society believes the engagement is a contrivance, however, I fear we are done for."

~

IN DESPAIR AND FRUSTRATION, Philip went directly from the attorney's office to his club. After his first scotch had been drained, he ordered another. Although he drank deeply, he found no relief at the bottom of his glass. A copy of the contract was folded in his inner coat pocket; he'd signed it, of course, since to do otherwise might cause the attorney and his father to suspect something was amiss. Nevertheless, the contract to purchase Grovebrook was about as useful to him as a perforated umbrella. He was not too drunk yet to see the irony in the situation. *Everything I attempt these days seems to backfire spectacularly.*

As Philip finished his second drink, Gryphon paused a few feet away to sneer.

"Drinking heavily, are we? You hardly look the part of a joyous fiancé. One would almost think your providential engagement to Miss Beaucroft was a farce." His self-satisfied smirk irritated Philip to no end. "Enjoy it while it lasts." The man strode off with a swagger.

Although Philip was mystified at the encounter, he knew a distinct threat when he heard one. Gryphon couldn't possibly know for certain his betrothal was a ruse...could he? A feeling of dread came over him suddenly, and he left the club to return to Trestlebury House. Prudence, who was hovering just inside the doorway to the drawing room, straightened when he walked through the door.

"There's Philip now!"

"What has happened?" he asked.

"You'd best go in," she replied.

His entire family had congregated in the drawing room, and

from the looks on their faces, he'd been the topic of conversation. His glance flickered toward Augustus, but his brother's pained, wooden expression gave him no clue.

"Is your engagement to Miss Beaucroft genuine or not?" Moregate demanded.

"What? Why would you ask such a thing?"

Augustus cleared his throat. "It seems someone has been circulating the rumor around town that your betrothal to Miss Beaucroft is merely a contrived distraction."

"Tell us the truth, Philip," Eve said. "This ugly accusation is threatening our respectability!"

"I assure you, my regard for Kitty is utterly genuine. I'd like nothing better than to make her my wife." As he spoke, Philip knew he'd answered from his heart. Pretending Kitty Beaucroft was his fiancée was the overwhelming reason he'd enjoyed the ruse so much.

A collective sigh of relief.

"I knew it!" Moregate said.

"So did I," Prudence said. "Anyone who sees Miss Beaucroft and Philip together can't deny their mutual affection."

"I agree, Prudence. To counteract these malicious rumors, we must move ahead with the wedding plans as soon as may be," Lady Moregate said. "A special license must be procured, and the arrangements made."

"The engagement party is a week from today. It can easily be turned into a wedding breakfast, if the special license can be expedited," Eve said.

"I'll use all my powers of persuasion," Moregate said. "It will be managed."

Prudence clapped her hands together. "How exciting! I do so love weddings."

"Wait just a minute," Philip managed. "Kitty wants a long engagement! It would be wrong to rush her."

"I discussed the matter at length with her father this afternoon, Philip," Augustus said. "He agrees the wedding cannot wait."

"Why? I'm not following you," Philip said.

"Lady Lovejoy snubbed me today," Eve said. "She knows simply everyone, Philip. Trust me on this; if she believes the rumors, everyone does. Until you and Miss Beaucroft actually wed, we're social pariahs."

Philip gave his brother a pleading glance, to no avail. If Augustus couldn't help him, he was indeed destined to wed an unwilling bride. *Kitty will hate me forever and there's nothing I can do about it.*

BEAUCROFT CALLED his family into the study and shut the door. "We have a situation, I'm afraid." He described the conversation at the cricket ground between him, Lord Ferndale, and Lord Elbourne.

"It's just silly gossip, Papa," Kitty said. "We needn't pay any attention."

"I thought not either until I conferred with your mother." Beaucroft nodded at his wife. "Tell her."

"I received three notes today, canceling upcoming events," Mrs. Beaucroft said. "I expect the events were not canceled at all, but that we were dropped from the guest list."

Kitty was bewildered. "I don't understand how our secret was discovered. Other than us, only Philip and his brother knew the truth!"

"It matters little since the damage is done. You and Lord Philip must wed as quickly as possible now," Beaucroft said.

Juliet cried, "No!"

"You must be joking, Papa," Kitty said. "There's no need for that."

"I'm perfectly serious. In fact, I urge you and Lord Philip to elope."

"Dearest, I respectfully disagree. An elopement would just add to the scandal," Mrs. Beaucroft said.

"Very true," Ivy said. "If there is an elopement, unflattering assumptions will be made regarding Kitty's virtue. I say we should schedule the wedding as quickly as possible and leave it at that. If preparations are being made publicly, the Beaucrofts should be able to regain some social standing."

Tears were streaming from Juliet's eyes, but all Kitty felt was numb. Decisions were being made about her future without any consideration of her feelings, and she felt as if her life was spinning out of control.

"Papa, I'm having difficulty understanding how you could have changed your mind about Philip on the basis of an idiotic rumor."

"In the hands of the vindictive, idiotic rumors can ruin even the most pious of souls," he replied. "The die is now cast."

"You don't understand. Lord Philip doesn't wish to marry me!" She dropped her face in her hands. "I'm so humiliated."

Watson tapped on the door. "Excuse the interruption, but Miss Beaucroft has a gentleman caller. Lord Philip Butler."

A wave of panic made Kitty gasp. "Oh, no, I can't possibly see him right now!"

"Shall I tell him you're not at home?" Watson asked.

Beaucroft cleared his throat. "Show him into the drawing room, Watson. Kitty, you cannot avoid him forever. Go hear what Lord Philip has to say."

As if she were headed to the guillotine, Kitty left the study. She walked down the hall, knowing Philip's manner toward her would undoubtedly be resentful. Would he blame her somehow for disclosing their ruse? Perhaps he would refuse to marry her at all!

When she entered the drawing room, he was standing in front of the fireplace, staring at the cold grate.

"Philip," she said. "I'm so sorry."

He looked up just as her composure crumbled. His expression was one of concern, with no trace of anger whatsoever. His arms opened wide, and she rushed into his warm, comforting embrace. Their words tumbled out in a rushing torrent of emotion.

"I'm the one who is sorry," he murmured. "Please don't hate me."

"I could never hate you."

"I hope you don't think I had anything to do with the rumors."

"Why would I? You've no motive."

"Oh, Kitty, you could do so much better than marrying me."

"You're wrong. I couldn't."

He pulled back, searching her face with his eyes. "What?"

"Perhaps you've no title or fortune, but I've never met a better man. If it weren't for the fact you're being forced into matrimony, I wouldn't have any regrets."

"If I thought you really meant it, I—"

"I do mean it, Philip. Despite the best of intentions otherwise, I've come to care for you deeply."

Kitty's pulse began to race when his lips claimed hers in a soft, tantalizing kiss that made her heart sing. Until that moment, she hadn't realized just how much she'd wanted him. She pulled him closer, wishing the kiss could go on forever. When his lips left hers to trail down her neck, pleasurable sensations sent shivers down her spine and throughout her body. She moaned, praying he wouldn't ever stop...

"Ahem," Ivy said.

They sprang apart, but Philip kept her hand tightly grasped in his. Ivy stood in the doorway of the drawing room, looking as if she'd bitten into a persimmon.

"I've been sent to see if all is well. I can see that it is."

A silly giggle. "Grandmama, allow me to introduce Lord Philip Butler, my wonderful fiancé."

WEDDING PREPARATIONS SPED along at a breakneck speed. Lord Moregate pulled strings and managed to procure the special license. Invitations for the engagement party were reissued as wedding breakfast invitations. With only minor alterations, Kitty's court presentation gown was fashioned into a wedding dress. Eagerly anticipating the moment when she would become Lady Philip Butler, Kitty floated through the days on a cloud of happiness.

The night before the wedding, Kitty waltzed around her bedchamber as if she'd had too much sparkling wine. Juliet laughed.

"Your wedding is tomorrow and you can't stop smiling. It seems you've overcome your fear of marriage."

"I've never been afraid of marriage. That notion was your own invention."

"I'm not so sure. Perhaps your regard for Philip has nullified your apprehension."

"My regard for him would nullify my apprehension, if I'd had any to begin with." Kitty stopped waltzing and collapsed into a chair. "Speaking of marriage, did Miss Haver announce her engagement yet?"

Juliet frowned. "An engagement? I haven't spoken to Violet recently, but I imagine she would have told me something of that importance."

"I spoke with Miss Haver briefly at Lady Lovejoy's ball. She mentioned her engagement to Lord Gryphon might soon be forthcoming."

"Lord Gryphon?"

"To be fair, he didn't look as if he enjoyed the prospect overmuch."

"No. I-I had no idea Violet was contemplating marriage, much less to him of all people. She's never even expressed any regard for the man."

"She can't be a very dear friend to conceal her feelings from you."

"No. No, she's not a good friend whatsoever." Juliet's voice was almost a whisper. "Forgive me, Kitty. I've been very mistaken in her character."

Juliet's face was pale, and she looked stricken. Kitty became concerned.

"You needn't ask my forgiveness. I'm just sorry she's hurt you."

She rang for a servant to bring her sister a strong cup of tea. While they waited for the tea, she took Juliet by the hand.

"I know this ruse with Philip has interrupted your Season dreadfully. As soon as I'm married, however, invitations will begin to arrive again. After tomorrow, all will return to normal, I promise."

She'd intended to cheer her sister up, but Juliet began to weep in earnest instead.

"You *do* love Philip, don't you?" she asked through her tears.

"Why, yes."

"And you truly want to marry him?"

"Of course. Juliet, tell me what's wrong?"

"Nothing. I'm fine."

Sobbing, her sister ran from the room. Moments later, Kitty heard Juliet's door slam shut. Mystified, she went in search of her mother. Mrs. Beaucroft was in the drawing room with Ivy, where the two women were filling out wedding breakfast place cards in elegant, flowing scripts.

"Mama, Juliet won't stop crying, and she won't tell me why."

"She ate very little at breakfast," Ivy said. "Perhaps she's hungry."

Mrs. Beaucroft sighed. "Weddings make everyone emotional. I've become teary-eyed a time or two myself."

She hastened from the room and up the stairs to tend to her daughter.

"Tell me, Kitty, does Philip have anywhere particular in mind for a honeymoon destination?" Ivy asked.

Kitty blushed. "Oh, er, he and I haven't discussed it actually. I imagine he's planning to visit Brighton or The Lakes."

"I thought you've always hated Brighton."

"I do, but if Philip likes Brighton, so shall I."

"My estate, Drake Manor, is quite near Grovebrook," Ivy said. "Why don't I stay in London, and you two may have the use of the place as long as you like? I'll send word to my servants to anticipate your arrival."

"That's uncommonly generous of you! Philip's very keen to see Grovebrook, and I expect he'd be delighted to accept."

"Good. I'll send Lord Philip the invitation straightaway. I think you'll find it easier to enter into the marriage state in somewhat familiar surroundings. Has your mother ever spoken to you about what a husband expects from a wife?"

"A little. If you're referring to managing a household—"

"No, I'm referring to matters of a more delicate and personal nature. I hate to speak of vulgarities, but there are things you ought to know. Nobody said a word to me when I was married, and it all came as quite a shock."

"Know what?"

"Sit down, Constance, and prepare yourself." She cleared her throat. "I hope you have a strong constitution."

TO WED OR TO WOE

*A*ugustus and Philip spent the afternoon at the tailor's shop, procuring suitable wedding clothes. While they were being fitted, Philip remembered the letter he'd received earlier that morning.

"I almost forgot to tell you. Mrs. Ivy Beaucroft has kindly offered me the use of her country house for the honeymoon. It's quite close to Grovebrook, so that will make it very convenient for me to get started with its management."

"I trust you won't spend all your time at Grovebrook and neglect your wife?" Augustus asked.

Philip laughed. "Most decidedly not. Kitty's grandmother sent a letter to her butler to inform him of our imminent arrival, but it's short notice. Therefore, we'll spend the wedding night at Trestlebury House and take the train north the following morning."

"I can't believe my younger brother is getting married before I am." Augustus shook his head. "I suppose after tomorrow the realization will have sunk in."

As their carriage approached Trestlebury House an hour

later, Augustus touched Philip's arm. "Isn't that Lord Kirkham, leaving the house just now?"

"I believe it is." Philip opened the window to wave. "Kirkham!"

His friend could not have failed to hear the greeting. Instead of acknowledging it, however, Kirkham mounted his horse and galloped off down the street.

"I wonder why he didn't wait?" Philip said, puzzled. "I wanted to make sure he would be at the wedding."

"He took off like the devil himself was in pursuit."

When they entered the house, raised voices were coming from Trestlebury's study. Philip exchanged an alarmed glance with Augustus.

"That can't be Prudence," Philip murmured. "She never shouts about anything."

"Sounds like she's having a row with her father."

Trestlebury stormed out of the study, stopping abruptly when he saw the brothers standing there.

"I'm off to my club for the evening. Perhaps one of you two can talk some sense into the girl."

He snatched up his hat from a table in the entryway and left the house.

Augustus grimaced. "I leave Prudence to you, old boy."

"Why me? She's closest to you in age."

"Yes, but Kirkham is your friend. Besides which, you're more facile with words than I am, and will undoubtedly handle things far better."

"Coward."

"Exactly."

Chuckling, Augustus made his way toward the stairs. Philip loosened his collar and entered the study. Prudence was pacing near the window, trembling with fury.

"Is everything all right, Pru?" he ventured.

She stopped pacing and glared at him instead. "This is all your fault!"

"What's my fault?"

"Papa has just refused his permission for Freddie to marry me."

"Oh. I'm very sorry, but how can it be my fault?"

"Originally, he and I were going to elope. After he spoke with you, however, he was convinced an elopement wouldn't be honorable."

"Well, I could hardly countenance my friend running off with my cousin, could I? This family is in enough trouble as it is, no thanks to me."

Tears glistened in Prudence's large brown eyes. "Philip, I'm nearly twenty-five years old. I'm no beauty. I'm not good with small talk, I read too much, and I speak my mind too often. Freddie loves me anyway. If I don't marry him, I'll never marry. And I love him most passionately."

"Would it help if I spoke with your father? I'd be happy to put in a good word about Kirkham."

"That will do no good. Although Mama is far more realistic about the situation, Papa seems to think a company of dukes will be vying for my hand any day now. I want you to go after Freddie and tell him you've changed your mind about the elopement. He respects your opinion."

"But I haven't changed my mind. An elopement will make you the subject of salacious gossip and supposition. I don't want that for anything in the world."

"I don't care! This is my last chance at happiness. Listen, Philip, I've known all along your engagement with Miss Beaucroft was a ruse."

He peered at her. "You have?"

"Of course! You're not the sort of man to give your heart to a girl you've only just met, not even one as pretty as Miss Beaucroft. Nevertheless, I kept your secret because I suspected the ruse would turn into a romance. I was proved correct, and now you must afford me the same courtesy."

"What would you have me do?"

"Freddie and I have the romance, but now we need a ruse. Papa has confined me to the house unless I'm in his company, and I'm not allowed to send or receive any correspondence unless he reads it first. I must find a way to escape so Freddie and I can elope to Scotland."

As Philip regarded his cousin, he suspected she'd correctly assessed her marriage prospects. She was a lovely person, but didn't possess the vivacious personality or wit necessary to overcome her distinct lack of conventional beauty. He and Kitty had railed against circumstances not of their making, so why should Prudence be any different? It was only the edicts of society which prohibited her from choosing a marriage partner beneath her in rank and fortune. Although his first instinct was to protect Prudence, what was he protecting her from, exactly? Kirkham was an honorable gentleman and a dear friend. Philip had nothing to fear regarding his intentions toward her.

"You could slip away during the wedding celebration tomorrow, when nobody is watching. Are you prepared to do that?" he asked.

"Yes."

"Please understand, your father may never forgive you."

"It's not important. If I don't marry Freddie, I'll never forgive my father."

A long sigh. "All right. Pack a small trunk with essentials. When you're done, I'll take it to Kirkham and arrange everything."

Prudence threw her arms around him. "Thank you, Philip! You've always been my favorite cousin."

VIOLET USHERED Lord Gryphon into the drawing room of her parent's home. Before she could speak, he produced a small packet of letters from his pocket and dropped them on a table. Her eyes widened. "My letters? Why are you returning them to me?"

"I see no reason we should continue our acquaintance."

Panic shot through her. "But I've done everything you asked! I blackened Lord Philip's and Miss Beaucroft's names to everyone of my association!"

"To no avail. Their wedding is to take place tomorrow." He sighed. "Our brief interlude was diverting enough, but it's become tedious. Let's not drag out the inevitable. I shall not be calling upon you again."

Her hand clutched his sleeve.

"You must marry me, Zachary! We've no choice now." She lowered her voice. "I've reason to believe I'm in the family way."

A sound of disgust. "How far along?"

She felt her face burn with embarrassment. "I'm three weeks late—perhaps four."

"Good. I know a woman who helps ladies extricate themselves from these difficult situations for a price. I can provide you with an introduction, if you like."

Violet recoiled. "No!" Moisture pooled in her eyes and spilled from the corners. "This is all your fault! We must go to Gretna Green and marry immediately."

He laughed. "What on earth would induce me to marry a girl who has been despoiled?"

"Please, Zachary! I thought you were a gentleman!"

"In that case, Miss Haver, you've been sadly mistaken." He bowed. "Good afternoon."

He strode from the room without a backward glance, and Violet collapsed onto the floor.

～

As Philip stood in the open doorway of Kirkham's apartment, his friend peered at the trunk in his hands. "You're not planning to move in, are you? The landlord only allows an occupancy of one in these lodgings."

"Move aside, Kirkham. This is rather heavy."

Philip brushed past him into the somewhat shabby apartment and lowered the trunk onto the floor with a thump.

"Do you still want to marry Prudence?"

"More than anything. I suppose you heard Lord Trestlebury refused my offer." His downcast expression matched the set of his shoulders.

"Prudence believes I discouraged you from eloping."

"You did, rather."

"After speaking with her, I've given it some thought and changed my mind. I want her to be happy, and I think you're the man for the job." He pulled a wallet out of his jacket. "I'd reserved this money for my honeymoon, but I won't be needing it. Kitty's grandmother is allowing us to use her house in the country."

"I can't accept this!"

"Yes, you can. Honestly, I don't know how Trestlebury will react when he realizes his daughter has run off. You two may have to take up residence in Scotland for some weeks. When you're ready, come visit Kitty and me in Grovebrook. You'll always have a warm welcome there."

"I-I don't know what to say, Butler."

"Say you'll take care of Prudence and treasure her, no matter what."

"I swear to you that I will. You've my word."

"Hire a carriage and be waiting for her across the street from Trestlebury House at eleven o'clock tomorrow morning. I advise you to get to the train station thereafter with all due haste, in case her absence is noticed too soon. Oh, and don't forget Prudence's luggage." He patted the trunk. "She won't be carrying anything when she slips away."

"I can't thank you enough, old boy." His grin faded. "Lord Trestlebury has forbidden me to come anywhere near his daughter, so I won't be at your wedding. That's my only regret."

"You'll be there in spirit." He shook Kirkham's hand. "Tomorrow, you and I will be two of the happiest men in England."

It was a beautiful day for a wedding. Kitty rode alone in an open carriage trimmed with fragrant flowers. People lined the street, waving and cheering as she passed. When driver turned around in his seat to give her an amused glance, she was shocked to realize it was Lord Gryphon.

"What are you doing here?"

"I'm here for the funeral," he said.

"What? It's a wedding, not a funeral."

"That's what you think."

The hem of her skirt became the color of pitch and spread upward until her entire dress was black. The horse pulled the carriage around the corner, and the church loomed into view. Kitty began to tremble.

"Stop the carriage! I want to get out!"

Gryphon merely laughed. "You should have thought of that earlier."

When they reached the church, Miss Haver was waiting out front, dressed in mourning. Gryphon jumped down from his perch and opened the carriage door. Hot tears spilled down Kitty's face, and she shook her head.

"This isn't what I'd anticipated at all. I don't want to die!"

Both Gryphon and Miss Haver howled with mirth. The bouquet in Kitty's hands crumbled, revealing the ropes snaked around her wrists. Four of her rejected suitors suddenly materialized. Along with

Gryphon, they seized the end of her rope and yanked her from the carriage.

"No!" Kitty exclaimed. "I'm not ready."

In the doorway of the church, Grandmama beckoned her forward. Although Kitty braced her legs against the cobblestone pavement, it was no use. As she was pulled inexorably forward, her throat began to burn with the strength of her screaming...

Something grabbed her shoulders and shook her.

"Kitty, wake up! You're having a nightmare," Juliet said.

Her eyes popped open. The light from a single candle barely lifted the darkness, but she could see her sister's face.

"I don't want to die. I mean, I don't want to get married." Kitty sat up. "I'll run away. I should have left London immediately after rejecting Lord Gryphon."

"Kitty, you've had a bad dream, that's all. Do you love Philip?"

"Yes."

"Does he love you?"

"I think so. Yes, I know he does."

"Then you can have nothing to fear, Kitty." Juliet sighed. "I thought you'd overcome all this."

"And so I had, until Grandmama arrived. I'd no idea—" She broke off, unwilling to repeat the things her grandmother had told her.

"These are modern times, and nobody will force you to marry Philip if you don't want to. But I've seen how happy you've been since your engagement became real. Do you really want to throw that away?"

"N-No."

"Concentrate on your feelings of love instead of the fear, and you'll be fine."

As Kitty pictured Philip's handsome face and trim figure, her heart melted.

"Yes. Yes, you're right. Nothing ill can happen when we're in love with each other." She smiled. "I'm the elder sister. I should be giving *you* advice."

"You've done so on many occasions, and will do so again in the future." Juliet stood and picked up the candle from the bedside table. "Now get some rest. You don't want to look tired in the morning."

"Thank you, Juliet. I'm sorry to have wakened you."

"You didn't. I haven't been sleeping well lately."

Kitty's sister left, and darkness descended once more. She fingered the Claddagh ring on her finger almost like a talisman. *Philip is my friend and would never do anything to hurt me.* She repeated that, over and over, until she managed to fall into a deep, restful slumber.

Philip's valet roused him from the few hours' sleep he'd managed to acquire. All night long he'd lain awake, worried about his impending nuptials. Would he make a good husband? The idea he was to be responsible for a wife's happiness and future was formidable, to say the least. All the reasons he'd vowed not to marry came back to haunt him in his final hours as a bachelor. He and Kitty both knew she could have married better. Despite their mutual affection, what if she came to regret their hasty union? On the other hand, he couldn't wait to make her his wife and hold her in his arms. His good fortune in marrying Kitty was a stunning turn of events by anyone's reckoning. If he'd already been in possession of an enormous fortune and could have had his pick of brides, he still would have chosen her.

He was fully dressed when Augustus tapped on his door.

"Coming down to breakfast?"

"Er...I'm not hungry."

Augustus laughed. "You look as pale as new milk. Have some tea and perhaps a piece of toast. I think you'll feel better."

Philip shot him a terse glance. "I'll remind you of that on your wedding day." He paused. "I hope you don't resent my marrying Kitty. You rather fancied her."

"Any dispiritedness I experienced soon passed. Now that I know her a little better, I realize she's far more compatible with you. In fact, I probably would have bored her silly with my butterfly collections and drawings. I may have mentioned, I was initially drawn to her sister. I should have followed my first instincts."

"Are you going to pursue Juliet?"

"She's quite young still, so we'll see how things develop going forward." His eyebrows drew together. "You know, it's a shame about poor Prudence. I daresay Trestlebury has made a grievous mistake in rejecting Lord Kirkham."

Although Philip's first impulse was to tell his brother of the planned elopement, he bit his tongue. If his cousins discovered Philip's complicity in the plot, he would likely receive the brunt of their rage. Better to keep Augustus ignorant and therefore blameless.

"I agree. Now let's see if I can eat something and keep it down."

Augustus chuckled and patted him on the shoulder. "I can't believe it. My intrepid brother has finally found something that frightens him."

"Weddings frighten any sane man."

WHILE BRIDGET DRESSED HER HAIR, Kitty sat at the vanity table and tried to remain calm. A myriad of last-minute details were flooding her mind, racing around like a litter of irrepressible puppies. A small trunk had already been delivered to Trestlebury House in preparation for her stay overnight. Several larger trunks filled with her belongings were stacked in the entryway downstairs. Those trunks were to be shipped to Drake Manor the following day and thereafter accompany her to Grovebrook. *In a very short while, my name will no longer be Beaucroft and the house I've resided in every Season since I was born will no longer be my home.* Her shiver of apprehension gave way to a stab of excitement. *At last I will be able to preside over my own household and have the freedom to do whatever I like!* Living in the country would hopefully have one distinct advantage over town: she wouldn't have to put up with the constant scrutiny of nosy gossips and deceitful acquaintances.

Juliet entered the room. "Oh, you look lovely! The carriage is here. Are you ready?"

Kitty's stomach leaped into her throat. "Give me a moment."

She twisted her Claddagh ring, said a quick prayer, and then joined her sister in the hallway. *It's Philip who is waiting for me at the church, not an ogre.* An unexpected giggle spilled out.

"What is it?" Juliet asked.

"I was just thinking...if it were Lord Gryphon I was to marry, I would have slipped out of the house last night and fled to France. But it's Philip. He told me once I had nothing to fear while he was around, and I trust him."

Juliet smiled. "I trust him too."

AN HOUR LATER, Kitty Beaucroft was Lady Philip Butler. Any apprehension she'd had on the way to the church disappeared when she stood next to Philip at the altar. On their private carriage ride to Trestlebury House afterward, he could not keep his eyes off her.

"I can't believe you're mine. You're so very beautiful."

When they kissed, his lips lingered in a slow, enticing caress that sent Kitty's mind reeling. His intoxicating taste, touch, and fragrance filled her senses, and she felt an overwhelming stirring at her center.

With a groan, Philip finally pulled away. "I suppose it's unseemly to ravish you before the wedding breakfast."

The delicious sensations he'd aroused were so enjoyable, Kitty had no trouble at all pushing her grandmother's talk from her consciousness.

"Oh, I don't know. Perhaps our guests could get along without us for a short while."

He laughed. "A proper ravishing takes time and undivided attention."

She blushed.

"Besides which, I don't intend to ravish you," he said. "What I have in mind is far, far more romantic."

Blissfully content, she leaned her head on his shoulder. *Perhaps Grandmama doesn't know everything about the marriage bed. I've been terribly silly to be so afraid.*

FOR BETTER OR FAR WORSE

As he handed his new wife down from the bridal carriage and escorted her into Trestlebury House, Philip couldn't stop smiling. He and Kitty formed a receiving line, and as guests began to arrive, he shook hands and responded to sentiments of well wishes. After what Eve had told him regarding Lady Lovejoy, he was somewhat surprised to see her in attendance, but he greeted her warmly. During the wedding breakfast festivities, Eve took him aside and confided the woman had called on her the previous day and apologized for her precipitous outburst.

"I was obliged to accept her apology, on Kitty's behalf," Eve said. "One can't afford the luxury of offending a woman as powerful as Lady Lovejoy."

"I suppose many naysayers will be surprised Kitty and I are wed."

"Indeed, and I hope they are suitably ashamed of themselves." Eve lowered her voice. "Thank you for your assistance to Prudence."

"I'm not sure what you mean."

"Yes, you are. She's told me everything. Now when the event

comes to light, say nothing. I intend to take complete responsibility for it."

"I can't let you do that, Eve."

"His lordship won't throw *me* out of the house, but he may very well vent his spleen on anyone else he believes to be culpable. Trust me; Daniel and I have been married for twenty-seven long years. I know best how to manage him and you don't. Just stay out of it."

"If you think it's for the best."

"I do."

"Kirkham is a splendid fellow."

"I agree. Perhaps someday I'll even be able to invite him here for dinner. Now go enjoy yourself, Philip. It's a joyous occasion."

He gave Eve a kiss on the cheek. "It's the happiest day of my life, actually."

KITTY'S GAZE rested on her handsome husband as he crossed the room toward her father. The two men exchanged a few pleasantries, then they stepped from the banquet room and out of sight. Juliet followed her look.

"I wonder where Philip is going with Papa?"

"I hope they don't intend to share a bottle of spirits," Kitty said.

"Surely not. Papa has never been much of a drinker. Perhaps a cigar?"

"I don't believe Philip smokes. Well, it's too late for Papa to withdraw his permission, so I suppose I'm safe."

They giggled. Despite her present merriment, Kitty noticed dark smudges underneath her sister's eyes. A creeping sense of guilt brought a slight frown.

"I'm so awfully sorry for waking you last night, Juliet. I left a present for you in my closet to make up for it."

"Tell me what it is!"

"A certain hat of mine you've been admiring these past two months."

"Not really?"

"Really. Truth be told, it suits you far better anyway."

"It does not, but I love you for saying so."

Kitty was relieved to see her sister's mood lift somewhat. Shortly thereafter, Philip and her father returned to the party. As Philip slid into the seat next to Kitty, he gave her a dazzling smile.

"What were you and my father talking about so secretively just now?" she teased.

"Oh…this and that. He threatened to beat me senseless if I didn't bring you breakfast in bed every morning, complete with a red rose."

"I never knew Papa was such a romantic."

Kitty knew he was concealing something, but she chose not to let it bother her. It was her wedding day, after all. Lady Trestlebury—Cousin Eve, now—had done a beautiful job arranging a sumptuous repast. The quartet of musicians in the corner was playing lively, happy music, and all was well. Trestlebury was drinking far too much, however, and it seemed to Kitty the servants were overly eager to fill his glass. The wine had a soporific effect, and the poor man began to nod off, even though it was only midday.

Lady Lovejoy beckoned her over for a chat.

"Eve tells me you're to honeymoon at your grandmother's estate, and thereafter reside in the country? I hope that doesn't mean we will be deprived of your company too long. I should like to take you under my wing."

"How very kind of you, Lady Lovejoy! I can't tell you with

any certainty when I'll be in town next, but I'll certainly call upon you when I am."

"I shall quite count on it, dear." She leaned closer. "All the best news finds its way to me first, you know, although recently I've learned a hard lesson about my sources. It was Miss Haver who insisted to me that your engagement was a ruse."

"Did she? That was unkind, but perhaps she was acting under Lord Gryphon's influence. I believe he harbors some ill will toward Philip and me."

"You're probably right, but Miss Haver claimed she heard it directly from Lord Philip himself, if you can believe such maliciousness. It goes without saying I've dropped her from my list. Curiously enough, I received her *pour prendre congé* card just this morning. She's gone off to the country to live with her great-aunt for some strange reason."

"Miss Haver is leaving town in the middle of the Season? How very unusual!"

A smug smile. "Indeed. I suspect she's been thrown over by Lord Gryphon and has gone off to recuperate. She dropped many hints in the last few weeks that their engagement was imminent, but I'm told the man embarked on a tour of the continent yesterday. He's a heartless cad if ever there was one."

Although Kitty was hard pressed to find compassion in her heart for the girl, she didn't say so. "Miss Haver will eventually realize she's far better off without him."

"Perhaps. There could, of course, be another less charitable explanation for Miss Haver's disappearance. Let's just say she wouldn't be the first silly girl spirited off to the countryside for nine months."

Before Kitty could react, Philip swooped down. "Forgive me, Lady Lovejoy, but I'd like to dance with my wife."

The older woman was all smiles. "I can't imagine such a thing, and at your own wedding too."

Kitty giggled and joined her husband on the dance floor. "Husband and wife. That sounds so droll."

"I'm getting used to it more easily than I'd anticipated."

Trestlebury woke up with a loud snort, and Kitty bit back a laugh.

"I see our host is awake," she said.

"Probably seeking dessert."

"Then we should cut the cake after this dance." She glanced around, puzzled. "I hope Prudence is well. She disappeared an hour ago without a word."

Philip averted his eyes. "She's as well as can be expected. Lord Kirkham was refused permission to marry her yesterday and banned from ever seeing her again. Prudence took it rather hard at the time."

Kitty's brow furrowed. "Oh, dear. I should go check on her."

"No, don't do that," he said quickly.

"Why ever not?"

"Er…I think she needs to be alone right now. Please don't worry."

For the second time that day, Kitty had the nagging suspicion Philip wasn't being completely straightforward with her. Nevertheless, she brushed it aside.

"I don't believe Lord Kirkham and I have ever been introduced. He's a close friend of yours, isn't he?"

"We're the best of friends, and he would have made Prudence a wonderful husband. Unfortunately, her father disagreed."

"What a shame. I want everyone to be as happy as we are right now." Suddenly Miss Haver and Lord Gryphon flashed into her mind. *Well, maybe not everyone.*

The cake was cut and pieces handed around, but Kitty became worried when Prudence had still not returned. Juliet approached and voiced the same concern.

"Prudence suffered a romantic setback yesterday, I'm told,"

Kitty said. "Philip thinks she wants to be alone, but I don't think it does any good for her to brood."

"Especially not when there's cake to be had."

"Especially not then."

"I'll pop upstairs and see if I can't coax her into coming down."

"That's a wonderful idea, Juliet. You've always had a knack for making people feel better."

Her sister hastened from the room. In the meantime, the first of the wedding guests began to take their leave. Ten minutes later, she noticed Juliet return with a letter in her hand and a worried expression on her face. She brought the letter to Trestlebury, who was laughing uproariously at a joke Mr. Beaucroft had told.

"Excuse me, Lord Trestlebury. I went looking for Prudence, but she's not in her room," Juliet said. "I found this letter on her bed, addressed to you."

Apparently Trestlebury was still feeling the effects of too much wine. He merely stared at the letter without opening it. "How extraordinary! Why would my own daughter write me a letter?"

To Kitty's surprise, Philip flinched and shot Eve a panicked look. Eve smiled as she leaned over to pluck the letter from her husband's hand.

"What the devil!" he exclaimed.

"You should take this into your study, dearest, and let Philip and Kitty tend to their guests."

Without waiting for a reply, Eve left the room with the letter, followed closely by Trestlebury. Kitty was bewildered but continued to thank her guests for coming. Her good-byes with her family were tearful as she embraced them for the last time in a long while.

"Remember what I told you, Constance," Ivy whispered. "Don't forget you're English and you'll be fine."

Kitty gulped. "Yes, Grandmama."

Juliet gave her a kiss. "What has happened to Prudence, do you suppose?"

"I don't know, but I'll send word to you when I find out."

No sooner had the last guest left when Trestlebury burst from his study, his face florid. "Somebody call the constable! Prudence has eloped!"

KITTY FINALLY MADE her way upstairs to the room she was to share with Philip. The aftermath of her wedding breakfast had certainly not gone the way she'd thought it would. After Trestlebury's shocking revelation, the ensuing commotion had inadvertently made her feel like an outsider. After a string of oaths and imprecations, Trestlebury became short of breath and a physician was summoned. Philip's father sent for the police and thereafter accompanied a policeman to the surrounding train stations to search for the eloping couple. Furthermore, although Augustus had been taken aback at the news, it seemed to Kitty that Philip had not registered the sort of surprise an unexpected elopement should have engendered. Philip had known of the elopement, Kitty was certain, but why had he kept the information from her? A tinge of annoyance crept into her thoughts. Didn't he trust her to be discreet? Hopefully this wouldn't lead to their first quarrel!

She entered the bedchamber, glad to be alone for a little while to compose herself. It felt strange to be occupying a room with a man's things hanging in the closet. The bed drew her focus for a long moment before she deliberately turned her back. *I cannot think about that just yet!* Bridget appeared to help her change from her wedding dress into a less formal gown. While the maid was fastening her buttons, Kitty's gaze focused on some papers on the table—the contract to purchase Grovebrook. She was eager to show interest in her husband's new project, so after Bridget took the wedding dress away, Kitty picked up the contract and sat down to read it. As her eyes darted across the page, her mind rejected what the words indicated. Three times she read the first paragraph, but she was unable to interpret it another way.

The sale of Grovebrook to Philip had been contingent upon his marriage to her.

Her blood ran cold. Before now, she'd assumed Philip had possessed no motive to disclose their secret, but the contract was proof that he had every motive in the world. *"It was Miss Haver who insisted your engagement was a ruse. She claimed she heard it directly from Lord Philip himself, if you can believe such maliciousness."* Kitty didn't want to believe it, but the evidence seemed conclusive. Philip had sent Miss Haver out to spread rumors of a false engagement, knowing the resulting social pressure would ultimately force the marriage to take place.

She pressed her fingertips to her temples to quiet the pounding.

Had Lord Gryphon been in on the plot the entire time too? How awfully convenient he and Miss Haver should both have left London before the wedding, distancing themselves from any probing questions. For further proof of Philip's mendacity, she need look no further than his concealment of Prudence's elopement. For all she knew, Lord Kirkham had targeted the poor girl in a scheme to get his hands on her inheritance, all with Philip's assistance. Tears stung Kitty's eyes, but she was determined not to cry. She must maintain a facade of strength and dignity when she confronted Philip, although to what end she was uncertain.

UNSETTLED AND ANXIOUS, Philip paced in the library while Augustus showed the physician out. When his brother returned, he shut the door behind him.

"It isn't Trestlebury's heart, is it?" Philip asked.

"No, the doctor believes it was a combination of stress and too much wine. Trestlebury has been confined to bed, and Eve is attending him."

Philip shook his head. "I'm so awfully sorry. I had no idea the fellow would take the news so hard."

"You knew?"

"Eve and I both knew. I suppose you could say I helped arrange it."

Augustus peered at him, aghast. "What the devil were you thinking? You've taken the man's hospitality, only to repay him with scandal and heartache? Badly done indeed."

"Prudence begged for my help and I couldn't refuse. You'd have done the same thing in my place."

"It was Trestlebury's considered judgment that Lord Kirkham wasn't good enough for his daughter. Who are you to substitute your opinion for his?"

His brother's rebuke stung more than Philip would have thought possible, and suddenly he was completely unnerved. Had his interference truly been ill-considered?

"I-I just...felt sympathy for Prudence's situation," he managed.

"Your sympathy should have motivated you to offer her a shoulder to cry upon, nothing more. I'm truly ashamed at what you've done."

The words whipped Philip across his soul and unleashed a wellspring of emotion.

"Augustus, you don't know what it's like to be considered inferior! You've always been entitled, and you always will be. Some of the rest of us aren't so lucky. Because of her looks and temperament, Prudence has never been accorded the sort of admiration she deserves. Today, I had the opportunity to help her achieve happiness. I accept your criticism and blame; your points are well taken. Nevertheless, I'm not sorry. If you'll excuse me."

Trembling with anger, Philip strode from the room and hurtled up the stairs. Kitty, at least, would take his side in this. As a woman, she would understand affairs of the heart much better than his brother. Before he entered their bridal chamber, he paused to compose himself. All day long he'd yearned for her tender caresses. His wife deserved a romantic wedding night, and despite his argument with Augustus, he intended to show her just how much she was loved. Perhaps the smile on his lips was forced at present, but once he saw Kitty's face, it would become genuine.

Philip tapped on the door and went inside. She was sitting by the window, staring out the glass, presumably consumed with worry for Trestlebury and Prudence.

"It's all right. Trestlebury is resting comfortably. I'm certain he'll be better tomorrow...physically at any rate." He loosened his collar. "I knew about the elopement, you may have guessed, and Augustus has taken me to task most severely for my interference." A pause. "I confess, his disapproval has thrown me off a bit."

Kitty remained silent and oddly still, as if she hadn't heard him.

"Prudence and Kirkham are very much in love, and when she asked for my help I couldn't refuse," he continued. "I hope you, of all people, don't blame me."

When Kitty turned to face him, he was shocked and alarmed at her cold, brittle expression.

"I read the Grovebrook contract," she said.

His eyes flickered to the papers he'd left on the table.

"Did you? Well, I'm glad. We're in the project together now, for better or worse."

"I had no idea the depths to which you would stoop, to trap me into marriage."

The breath left his lungs. "What?"

"Your ownership of the property was contingent upon our wedding taking place."

"Yes, my father insisted. What can that have to do with anything?"

"It provides me with your motivation, Philip. Lady Lovejoy unwittingly gave the game away at the wedding breakfast. I'm given to understand you told Miss Haver of our secret and she took it directly to one of the most influential women in society."

Her accusation sent him reeling. "Kitty, I swear I did no such thing!"

"It was a marvelous scheme, really. Your pretense about wishing to remain a bachelor was well played. And it's not difficult to imagine why you assisted Lord Kirkham in eloping with Prudence. The both of you have so much to gain in different ways."

A numbness crept across Philip's face and down his chest, making it difficult to speak. "Why would you convict me without even listening to what I have to say? I'm in love with you."

"You feel some regard for me, I understand, but you knew I would never marry a man so entirely beneath me unless I was obliged to do so. Miss Haver said you were a fortune hunter, but I ignored her warning."

Philip's world was crashing in on him, but something perverse in his nature made him laugh. Deep down, he'd always known Kitty thought him beneath her, but to hear her voice the truth ripped his very soul to shreds. Furthermore, she couldn't care for him at all if she'd judged him on the slimmest of evidence. Apparently, his beloved wife was trapped in a marriage to a man she didn't respect, and the only noble course of action would be to free her as much as possible—no matter what it cost him personally.

As if he were playing a role in a melodrama, he replied in the coolest tone possible. "Well, Kitty, you've found me out. Clever girl."

His movements felt wooden as he crossed to the closet, extricated his valise, and threw his things inside. He remembered to slip the contract on top before he closed the clasp with a snap.

"Where are you going?" She answered her own question. "To seek a warm wedding night welcome in the East End, no doubt."

Philip bit back an angry retort. "Let us understand one another going forward. Since you consider me a villain of the highest order, I release you from any obligation you have as my wife. We're legally married, true, but you may do as you like without any interference from me. The only thing I ask is that you not bring another man's child into the world while I'm alive."

She gasped. "How dare you!"

"Forgive me if I've given any offense." He departed quickly, before she could see the tears of regret and pain in his eyes.

Downstairs, he stopped in the empty drawing room and downed half a glass of whisky. Thus fortified, he left Trestlebury House, hailed a cab, and drove to his gentleman's club on Pall Mall. Although it wasn't too late to catch a train to Grovebrook, he was in no mood to travel. He intended to spend the night in one of the private rooms, get stinking drunk, and leave London the following morning.

After Philip obtained a room key at the desk, he bumped into an acquaintance, an older man whose name escaped his memory.

"Oh, excuse me, sir. I didn't see you standing there."

"Lord Philip Butler?" The man peered at him. "Why, isn't it your wedding night, lad?"

Blood rushed to Philip's face and turned the tips of his ears into twin flames of embarrassment. "Er...yes. Sort of."

The man chuckled, patted him on the shoulder, and leaned closer to whisper.

"Trust me, I completely understand. On our wedding night, my wife cried and locked me out of the bedroom. Don't worry, it's only nerves, and more common than you'd think. The lady will come around."

"Th-Thanks."

As Philip walked down the hall toward his room, jaw was clenched so tightly he thought his teeth might crack. He barely managed to maintain his composure until he closed the door behind him. Then, when he was alone, it was as if he would never be happy again.

FOR A FULL TEN minutes after Philip disappeared, Kitty was too stunned and angry to do anything but fume. Her husband had admitted his culpability without a qualm and then thrown off the yoke of matrimony as if it had meant nothing at all! How dare he admit he was heading to an East End brothel, or suggest she was free to commit adultery herself? The horror was beyond imagining. Perhaps she could get the marriage annulled...although she'd heard annulments were notoriously difficult to obtain. Truly, her situation was unbearable. Not only did Philip have Grovebrook, but he had her dowry as well!

One thing was certain, she was not going to spend the night in a bridal bed for one. Kitty rang for her maid.

"Lord Philip and I have had a change of plans. Please pack my trunk. I'm going back to my parents' house."

"Yes, milady."

While the maid worked, Kitty sat at the desk and wrote her

new cousins and in-laws a letter of explanation for her departure:

Forgive me for not conveying my sentiments in person, but I don't wish to intrude any further upon your privacy in a time of crisis. My plans with Philip have changed, and I find I must return to the bosom of my family for a little while. Please accept my heartfelt thanks for the lovely wedding breakfast. I could not have imagined a more beautiful event. I shall write again when I understand more fully how the future will unfold.

With Love,

Kitty

After sealing the envelope, Kitty went downstairs and left it on the vestibule table. She asked the butler to hail a cab, but then she was too restless to wait.

"I'm going on ahead. Bridget is packing my things. Could you send someone upstairs to bring my trunk down when she's finished?"

"Yes, Lady Philip."

Kitty set off down the street on foot. A block later, her pace slowed and a crushing sense of loneliness descended. She fancied herself in love with Philip. No, it was more than a fancy. She was absolutely in love with him. His touch had turned her insides molten, and his kisses had made her hunger for more. Philip had shown himself to be a swine, so why couldn't she turn off her feelings like a water tap?

A blister began to form on the back of her heel as she trudged along in the late afternoon heat, and a trickle of sweat ran down her spine. How could a person soar to the heights of ecstasy and into the depths of despair in the space of a few hours? Her lower lip trembled, but she was determined to remain stoic in front of her family. *How humiliating; I must confess to being an idiotic fool taken for everything by a fortune-hunting bounder!* Her dignity gone, the only thing she'd kept intact that day was her virtue—now utterly and completely useless for all intents and purposes. Her grandmother, at least, would be relieved.

The butler managed to keep his countenance when she arrived home, somewhat bedraggled.

"Lady Philip! My most hearty felicitations on your wedding today." He peered over her shoulder. "Will Lord Philip be arriving soon?"

"No, but my trunk and Bridget will be coming by cab momentarily. Is my father at home?"

"Yes, milady."

"Will you tell him I've come, please?"

Kitty entered the drawing room, where Juliet, her mother, and Ivy were sitting. Her sister squeaked with surprise.

"What are you doing here?"

"I need to speak with Papa." She sank onto a sofa and removed her hat. "You'll be interested to know Lady Prudence eloped during the wedding breakfast with a young man by the name of Lord Kirkham."

"So that's why she disappeared?" Juliet asked. "Merciful heavens!"

Beaucroft hastened into the room, his face etched with concern. "Is everything all right, child?"

"No. I've left Philip."

"He hurt you, didn't he?" Ivy's question sounded more like a statement.

"*No*, Grandmama. Not physically at any rate. Philip admitted he was responsible for disclosing our secret to Violet Haver, counting on her to gossip about it. He knew if our ruse was common knowledge, I would be forced into marriage to save my reputation. The sale of his property was contingent upon our marriage, you see. After I confronted him with what I'd learned, he gave me my freedom and left. He's a fortune hunter, Papa."

"That makes no sense at all." Beaucroft's face crinkled up in bewilderment. "Didn't he tell you about your dowry?"

"Tell me what?"

"At the wedding breakfast, he directed me to put the dowry in your name. I argued with him about it, but he said under the circumstances, he felt quite strongly you should be financially independent."

"What? He can't have done, Papa. No man would ever refuse a dowry."

"I can assure you, it's no mistake."

"Oh, Kitty, this is all my fault." Juliet's voice sounded strangled. "Philip didn't tell Violet anything about the ruse. *I* did."

"It couldn't have been you!"

"She goaded me into saying something I shouldn't have at Lady Lovejoy's ball. It was an accident, and I was too ashamed of myself to tell you afterward. If Violet said she had her information from Philip, it was a poisonous lie. I'm so awfully sorry!"

The roaring in Kitty's ears drowned out anything else anyone said after that, and the magnitude of her mistake hit her like an Arctic blast from a winter storm. By any measure, the things she'd said to her husband were unforgivable, and she'd thrown away any chance they'd had of happiness…without thinking twice. She dropped her face in her hands and began to sob. *Oh, Philip, what have I done to you?*

GROVEBROOK

*P*hilip gazed through the window as the train headed north, more to avoid making conversation with the passengers in his compartment than out of any real interest in the view. The weather was overcast and drizzly, which served to underscore his black mood. He knew it was far too early to gain any sort of perspective on the prior day's tragedy, but his alcohol-soaked brain couldn't stop obsessing about it anyway. Why Kitty had been so eager to believe the worst of him was unclear. She'd taken bits and pieces of information and woven them together in a damning case without giving him the benefit of the doubt.

To be sure, they'd had only a few scant weeks together—far too short a time to build a solid foundation of trust and respect. *We simply didn't know each other well enough to marry.* Perhaps after the euphoria of the wedding and subsequent celebration had ebbed, the reality of Kitty's situation had finally sunk in. When faced with the prospect of being wed to the lowly Lord Philip Butler, she'd spurned him. It was all completely understandable to an outside observer, but to Philip, however, the rejection had been a crushing blow. Every doubt and insecurity he possessed was magnified a thousandfold, until even the act of getting out of bed that morning had been arduous.

His argument with Augustus hadn't helped. In fact, Philip suspected he would have been far more persuasive with Kitty if he hadn't allowed his elder brother to get under his skin. Unfortunately, there'd been more than a kernel of truth in Augustus' accusations. It seemed he was always getting into scrapes because of his interference with things which were none of his concern. He found it difficult to let injustices pass when it was in his power to address them. Had he been a lesser man, he would have walked away from Gryphon's assault of Kitty at the Trestlebury ball. *I could have avoided a great deal of trouble by doing so, but I wouldn't have been able to live with myself.* Well, as a result of trying to do the right thing, he was now completely alone and married to a woman who wanted nothing to do with him. It was ironic, but hardly amusing.

He was weary and dispirited by the time he reached his destination—a train station in a small town a few miles from Grovebrook. Since he hadn't consumed anything all day, he ate a light meal at a small tavern across the street and then rented a horse at the stable. Fortunately, he had only his valise to carry, so he tied it onto the saddle and set off down the road. No rain had moistened the ground here, and the late afternoon sun was at his back. The closer he drew to Grovebrook, the more rutted and uneven the dirt road became. Philip was obliged to slow his horse's pace lest the beast break a leg. Annoyed, he wondered why his father's man of business—*his* man of business now— had allowed the road to fall into such disrepair. His first task would be to take Mr. Pratt to task.

The signpost for Grovebrook was so faded and obscured by bushes, he nearly overlooked it. As he entered the town, he had difficulty squaring the idyllic memory in his mind's eye with the appalling reality spread out before him. What was once a charming and quaint village was now a run-down and neglected ghost of its former self. Shops were vacant, with not so much as a *For Let* sign in their windows. Shingles were missing from rooftops, and one of the buildings had been obviously destroyed by fire somewhat recently. The faint scent of ash lingered in the air, and the ruins had been left to collect rain, mold, and mosquitos. Philip was so astonished, he reined in his horse to take it all in. For the first time that day, he was grateful Kitty wasn't there. He would have been utterly humiliated to present her with such a miserable wedding present. *It's obvious why Father received no offers to purchase Grovebrook, and what I agreed to pay was far too generous by half.*

He made his way to Mr. Pratt's address, a two-story cottage located at the far end of town. After he lifted the door knocker for the third time, however, he realized no one was going to respond. It was odd, to say the least, since it was nearing the dinner hour. In addition, although Mr. Pratt and his wife—if he had one—might be out, one of the servants should have at least opened the door to take his calling card. He circled around back, but the cottage was locked up. A peek through one of the windows revealed sheets over the furniture. The cottage was vacant.

Movement in a small orchard to one side of the house caught his eye. A young lad was gathering apples and stuffing them into a knapsack. Philip waved and shouted.

"Hullo there!"

The boy gasped and bolted. In his haste, he fell flat on his face, spilling his bounty on the ground. Philip strode over to help him to his feet.

"Are you all right?"

"Yeah." He hung his head. "Are you going to tell me mum I was scrumping?"

"No, but I have a question for you. Do you know where Mr. Pratt has gone?"

"Moved into the manor house."

"Did he?" His temper flared at the news, but he was careful to keep his countenance. Mr. Pratt was no more entitled to occupy the Grovebrook manor house than Philip was free to occupy Buckingham Palace. "When did that happen?"

"Been 'bout a year now, I reckon. Living all high and mighty he is, but these apples won't pick themselves."

"Then you're doing the owner of this property a favor, aren't you?"

"That would be Lord Marbles, innit? He owns everything around here."

A chuckle. "Lord *Moregate*, you mean. No, the town's been sold, just yesterday, to Lord Philip Butler. That's me." As he spoke, he felt a surge of pride. *Grovebrook might not be much, but it's mine.*

The boy's eyes opened so wide with surprise, Philip had to laugh. "What's your name, lad?"

"Pig."

"What?"

"Well, my real name's Nelson, but everyone calls me Pig."

"I hope you don't mind if I call you Nelson? You look more like a boy than a pig to me."

"You can call me anything you want so long as you don't tell me mum about the apples."

"Don't worry, Nelson. In fact, I'm appointing you my unofficial groundskeeper for this orchard until I hire myself a new man of business to occupy this cottage."

"Are you sacking Mr. Pratt?"

"Most definitely."

"Good. Me mum says he's a lazy, no-good, conniving scoundrel."

"Your mother sounds quite intelligent. Who's the constable around here?"

The freckled skin on Nelson's face turned pink underneath the dirt. "That would be me father."

"Lead me to him, will you? I've a scoundrel to evict."

Philip helped the boy retrieve his spilled apples, and was rewarded by an irrepressible grin. "I'm glad you've come, milord."

"Thank you. And tell your mother things will get better around Grovebrook in short order, I promise."

AUGUSTUS CALLED ON THE BEAUCROFTS, but the butler informed him the family wasn't receiving visitors. Just as he was turning away from the door, he heard Miss Juliet's voice.

"Is that Lord Elbourne? Please show him in."

As he entered the drawing room, he could see Juliet was under a strain.

"I'm sorry no one else is available to receive you. It's as if we're all in mourning."

"It's the same at Trestlebury House, although no one has covered the mirrors," Augustus said. "Prudence is married and living in Scotland for the time being. Trestlebury is in high dudgeon." He paused. "How is Kitty?"

"She's shut herself up in her room and won't come out. We're all worried about her. How is Philip?"

"He wrote Father to say he was in Grovebrook, but nothing else. We're worried about him, too." He paused. "Truth be told, I feel some responsibility for whatever happened between him and Kitty. After the wedding breakfast, Philip and I argued. He'd assisted Prudence and Kirkham with their elopement, you see, and I was quite angry with him about it. Under the circumstances, I probably should have held my tongue. Whenever we quarreled as children, he always took it very badly."

"Oh, Augustus—I mean Lord Elbourne—it's all my fault!"

Tears began to fall faster than she could brush them away, and he offered her his handkerchief and an encouraging smile.

"Please do call me Augustus. I'm your brother-in-law, after all."

"You won't want to speak with me after you hear what I have to say. *I* was the one who exposed the ruse. I didn't mean to, but I did. Then Kitty mistakenly blamed Philip for it and he left! I can never forgive myself!"

Augustus sat next to Juliet and covered her hand with his. When someone cleared their throat in the drawing room doorway, he snatched his hand away and sprang to his feet. He expected to be taken to task for his small liberty, but Ivy merely crossed into the room and sat on the sofa.

"I couldn't help but overhear how everyone is taking blame for what has happened between Kitty and Philip." She sighed. "I suppose I ought to take a double helping of blame myself."

Juliet stopped crying long enough to stare. "What are you talking about?"

"I think I may have frightened Kitty out of her wits on the eve of her wedding. Like you, Augustus, I should have held my tongue. Sometimes people who are frightened have been known to lash out at others. Certainly I've been known to do so upon occasion. If Kitty spoke sharply to Philip, I may have inadvertently set the stage."

"Perhaps we all contributed to this tragedy in different ways. The question now is what can we do about it?" Augustus asked.

"There's very little we can do, unfortunately. The two of them are going to have to find their way back to each another," Ivy said.

"What if they don't?" Juliet asked.

Ivy nodded. "In that case, I'll just have to give Kitty a little shove."

∼

DINNER THAT NIGHT at Trestlebury House was a sober affair as Augustus revealed what he'd learned about the rift between Philip and Kitty.

"I was worried their marriage wouldn't thrive, but I could never have imagined it would be over so soon," Lady Moregate said.

"It's not over yet," Augustus said.

"If it is, Philip deserves it," Trestlebury said.

Lady Moregate was taken aback. "That's quite a harsh sentiment."

"I agree, Daniel," Eve said. "I pray whatever happened between Kitty and Philip is resolved soon."

"Prudence could have married a duke!" Trestlebury pounded the table on every other word. "But because of Philip, she's run off with a worthless viscount. I can assure you, neither Kirkham nor my daughter will receive a penny from me. Moregate, I hold you directly accountable for having raised an interfering lout!"

"Now see here!" Moregate bristled. "Philip may be many things, but he's not a lout."

"I'd expect you to take up for him!"

Augustus held up a quelling hand. "Although I disagreed with my brother's actions, they were hardly malicious. Philip was quite sincere in wishing for Prudence's happiness."

"It was none of his concern!"

"Apparently, her happiness was none of yours, either," Eve said.

"Furthermore, I must be allowed to speak for Lord Kirkham," Augustus continued. "I'm well acquainted with the lad, and he's a gentleman of the highest caliber. I hope at some point you will come around."

"Never. He's not welcome in my house, and neither is your brother," Trestlebury said.

"You don't mean that, Daniel," Eve said, aghast. "You've allowed grief to cloud your judgment."

"I do mean it. Philip is *your* cousin by blood, not mine, which explains why you're all flocking together."

Everyone visibly recoiled.

"I'm afraid if my son isn't welcome in your home, then neither am I." Moregate's tone was quiet. "I thank you very much for your hospitality, Trestlebury, but my wife and I shall be departing in the morning."

Eve's lower lip trembled. "I believe I could use a little country air myself. I'll accompany you, if you don't mind."

"You're more than welcome to stay as long as you like, Eve." Lady Moregate took a deep breath. "If in the future you can find a little Christian charity in your heart, Daniel, you'll be welcome to join us."

Trestlebury harrumphed. After Lord and Lady Moregate filed out of the dining room with Eve, Augustus gave Trestlebury a level stare.

"I had believed Philip's interference to be officious, but I'm beginning to wonder if my grasp of the situation was incomplete." Augustus stood. "I'll be moving to my club until I find more permanent accommodations in town. I understand you need time to adjust to what has happened, but I urge you to reconsider your position. Whether or not you care about us, your family cares about you."

As he followed his parents and cousin from the room, Augustus shook his head. He'd had no idea how intractable Trestlebury could be. *It seems I owe Philip a sincere letter of apology.*

Ivy burst into Kitty's bedchamber and threw back the curtains. Sunlight suddenly flooded the room, and Kitty groaned in pain.

"Let's have no more of this nonsense," Ivy said. "You've been brooding in here for far too long." She sniffed the air and made a face. "From the smell of it, I don't think you've changed your clothes or bathed in a fortnight."

"There's no point," Kitty muttered. "My life is over, and I'm past caring about anything."

"Ridiculous! We've all made mistakes in life, but we don't just lie down and die! I thought you had more spine than this, Constance."

"I hurt the finest gentleman I've ever known, Grandmama. I can never take back what I said, and he'll never forgive me!"

"I believe you'll find he can, but not if you go to him dirty, bedraggled, and in need of a handkerchief." She peered at Kitty's unbrushed, tangled hair. "I shudder to think about getting a comb through that rat's nest."

Kitty sat up and gave Ivy a baleful look, which she ignored.

"I'm going to ring for the maid to draw you a bath and get you dressed. After you've had breakfast, you're coming with me to Drake Manor."

"I'm not hungry and I just want to sleep."

"Your cheeks are sunken, your pallor is horrendous, and you've eaten nothing for days on end. How do you expect to win back your husband if you can't even fill out your gowns properly? There's only so much padding can do."

Tears began to leak from Kitty's eyes, and she didn't bother to wipe them away. "I don't know where Philip is, Grandmama! I may have driven him into the arms of another woman."

"We've heard from Lady Moregate regarding a letter Philip sent just yesterday. He's in Grovebrook."

Ivy sat on the bed next to Kitty and took her hand.

"Listen to me, Constance. My husband was a despicable, self-centered brute, but my father forced me to marry him because he was rich. Not a day went by I didn't hate Mr. Beaucroft. If truth be told, I believe his son—your father— hated him too. You're extremely fortunate to have married a man of character. I like Lord Philip. I didn't expect to, but he won me over. Now prove you have what it takes to deserve him."

"I don't know if I can face him, Grandmama!"

"It will be difficult, I grant you, but you'll persevere. I'm determined to see you happy." Her expression grew apologetic. "Now that I've met Lord Philip, I'm not wholly convinced what I told you about the intimate side of marriage applies."

Kitty was taken aback. "You think not?"

"He adores you, child. If my husband had ever had any regard for me or my feelings whatsoever, I daresay I would have been more—" she cleared her throat "—enthusiastic about the process."

Ivy pulled the bell cord to call the maid. "Now, get out of bed and make yourself presentable. We've a ten o'clock train to catch."

PHILIP RODE his horse alongside the road, surveying the progress made in its reconstruction. He beckoned to the supervisor, who hastened over.

"Is the work proceeding to your satisfaction, milord?"

"Tell your men there's a substantial bonus in it for them—and for you—if they finish the work in two days. Is it doable, in your estimation?"

"Aye, if we work overtime."

"Is that a problem, Mr. Andrews?"

The lines in the man's weathered skin creased when he smiled. "No, milord, weather permitting. We can use a bit of extra money around here, if truth be told."

A nod. "Good. See to it."

On his way back through Grovebrook, Philip paused at the wreckage of the burned building, where several men were busy removing debris and draining the standing water. He would have dearly loved to rebuild the structure immediately, but until the other shops were filled with tenants, there was no point. A brief examination of the books had revealed evidence Mr. Pratt had been cheating his father for years. A lack of supervision had emboldened the man to mismanage Grovebrook, driving some tenants away and alienating the remainder. A notice for another man of business had been sent to the London papers, but it was too soon for replies. Patience had never been one of Philip's virtues, but he had to remind himself steady progress was better than none at all. Mr. Pratt had been sent packing without a letter of reference, at least, and some long overdue repairs were underway. Admittedly, an argument could be made Philip was doing too much too soon, but the relentless pace helped keep his mind off his own agonizing loneliness.

He returned home to the manor house, where an extensive overhaul was underway. He'd hired a temporary staff to remove all evidence of its most recent occupant and to clean the structure from top to bottom. The state of the garden alone had sickened him. Groundskeepers were busy clipping neglected hedges, pruning overgrown bushes and trees, and cutting the weed-choked grass. The large, stately home was lovely, however, with a classical, handsome pink sandstone exterior that had retained the beauty he remembered from his childhood.

The blacksmith was affixing a new nameplate onto the building next to the doorway when Philip arrived. After handing off his horse to a groom, Philip went to admire the blacksmith's handiwork.

"Thank you for your prompt installation, Mr. Franklin." He handed the blacksmith a quantity of pound notes. "I think that brings us up to date?"

"Yes, sir." He folded the notes into his pocket. "I'm grateful for the work, milord."

"Now that you mention it, there's a rotting wooden sign just outside Grovebrook that needs replacing with something more permanent. Perhaps a prominent iron plate set in a brick or stonework column?"

Mr. Franklin's face lit up, as if with inspiration. "I'll draw up a few designs for you. After you approve one of them, I can get started."

"I look forward to seeing your designs."

The blacksmith gave the newly installed plaque—marked CONSTANCE HALL—a final swipe with a clean cloth. "Does the name Constance have any special significance, if you don't mind me asking?"

Philip swallowed hard. "Constance is the Christian name of my wife, Lady Philip."

"I didn't know you were married, sir! Will we have the pleasure of milady's company soon?"

"It's quite unlikely. My wife vastly prefers town over country life." He forced a smile. "Good day to you."

Philip continued inside the house, which smelled of soap and polish. The windows and doors were open to allow the place to air out, and the streaming sunshine illuminated dust motes raised by an army of scullery maids. Mr. Pratt had left the house in a wretched condition, but Philip had made one providential discovery: a very fine collection of wine had remained untouched in the locked cellar for decades. Fortunately, Philip's father had given him the keys to the house, outbuildings, and cellar on his wedding day. To pay for the extensive repairs he'd undertaken, Philip had been obliged to sell many pieces of furniture, a few paintings, and most of the wine collection to a London merchant.

He lit a lantern and brought it down into the cellar. The racks in the back were empty now, but he'd still retained more wine than he could drink in a year or longer. After selecting a bottle, he brought it with him to the library, the one room into which Pratt had not bothered to venture. After the library had been dusted and aired out, the oak-paneled, majestic space had become Philip's private retreat. He opened the bottle of wine, poured himself a glass, and sat staring out into space. Suddenly his laughter filled the room, and he found he couldn't stop until a lack of breath forced him to fall silent. He'd acquired the property he so desperately craved, and married his ideal woman, yet he was destined to be alone for the rest of his life.

Now I understand the concept of Hell.

Kitty, Ivy, and their lady's maids arrived at Drake Manor before teatime. As the carriage rolled to a stop, Kitty felt a little strange being back at her grandmother's house after such a long absence. The estate had been a frequent summertime destination in her childhood. Her grandfather had passed away when she was a baby, so she had no recollection of the churlish disposition Ivy had described. If her father's frequent foul moods were any indication, however, he'd inherited a streak of the man's nasty temperament. *Of course, after my ill treatment of Philip, I'm in no position to throw stones at anyone.*

She was puzzled when Ivy directed the butler to leave her many trunks in the entryway.

"Why not have them taken to my room, Grandmama?" she asked. "My maid should press and hang up my gowns."

"You'll only need one," Ivy replied. "You'll not be staying long."

"I've just arrived! You can't be serious."

"You're to join your husband in Grovebrook as soon as the bloom is back in your cheeks. In fact, why don't you take a walk right now? Enjoy the fresh air while I confer with the cook about your diet. We'll have tea when you return."

Realizing Ivy would brook no opposition, Kitty threw up her hands in defeat. Outside, gravel crunched underneath her boots as she first crossed the courtyard and then stepped onto the velvety green lawn. Although she was loath to admit it to her grandmother, it felt good to stretch her legs after being cooped up on trains and carriages the entire day. In fact, she'd spent the better part of the past two weeks curled up in bed, feeling sorry for herself.

Her tour took her around the chestnut tree on the south side of the property and back toward the garden, where many fond memories brought a faint smile. She and Juliet used to play here once upon a time. They'd even had tea parties with their dolls in the wisteria-covered gazebo. As she sank down on a stone bench to enjoy the fragrant floral perfume lingering in the air, she wondered what Philip was doing at that moment. Could he sense she was nearby? A stab of pain brought a fresh round of tears to her eyes. *I'm such a fool. These past weeks we could have been here together, happy, on our honeymoon.*

Enough! She stood so abruptly, she nearly hit her head on a low-hanging branch. *I'm tired of crying. Grandmama is right; I need to find my spine. Philip has every reason to hate me, but I must accept the blame and move forward. I'll beg his forgiveness and win him back if it's the last thing I do.*

Her shoulders were squared and her chin was lifted as she entered the house. She found her grandmother in the drawing room.

"You must have had a nice walk," Ivy said. "Your complexion is much improved already."

"I did, thank you. When is tea? I'm quite hungry."

Ivy gave her a pleased look. "That's my girl."

Of course, Kitty began to doubt her resolve as her grandmother's beauty and health regimen began to unfold. Ivy ordered the cook to incorporate clotted cream and delicious, sweet butter into almost everything on Kitty's plate, including such dishes as scrambled eggs and mashed potatoes. Ivy also insisted she partake of regular exercise, whether she felt like it or not. Every morning Ivy pushed Kitty out the door to walk around the grounds, and every afternoon, she went riding. To make her skin glow, she choked down a teaspoon of cod liver oil before breakfast. Admittedly, being pampered wasn't all bad. After dinner, Bridget applied peaches and cream beauty masks to her face, followed by dabs of almond oil. Her scalp received a nightly massage, and her hair was conditioned with an aloe vera concoction. An olive oil bath for her nails promoted their growth.

Kitty cooperated as best she could, and slowly but surely, she became stronger.

OUT OF TUNE

Philip stared at the scorched porridge his cook set before him. The woman must have noticed his hesitation because she put her hands on her ample hips.

"Is something amiss?"

"Er, no. It's just…do you suppose we could change breakfast up a bit one of these days? Perhaps eggs, bacon, and toast, for a start?"

Her lips pursed. "It was good enough for Mr. Pratt." She untied the strings of her apron. "You've got my notice."

"I beg your pardon?"

"I'm not used to cooking fancy, milord. It's just too much."

She swept from the room with her nose in the air. He sighed and sat back in frustration. Mrs. Trench wasn't much of a cook, but she was the only one he had. Running Constance Hall had been more problematic than he'd anticipated. After the place had been cleaned, he'd hired several local women as maids. Unfortunately, without a housekeeper to keep order, they'd quarreled with one another and all but one had quit. The groundskeepers and groom were satisfactory, but the house was in dire need of a butler. In addition, Philip had felt the lack of a valet more than he thought possible.

Mrs. Trench appeared, wearing her hat and coat. "I'll have my wages now, if you'd be so kind."

Philip set out coins on the tablecloth, and she swept them into her hand. She regarded him a long moment before making a sound of exasperation.

"I'm going to do you a favor because you're much nicer than Mr. Pratt. Mr. Horn would make you an excellent cook, I'd wager. He had a lovely restaurant in Grovebrook before it burned to the ground."

"Was the food any good?"

"I heard tell it was, but I could never afford to eat there myself. I understand Mr. Horn learned his trade at some fancy London hotel."

"Er…what caused the fire?"

"Weren't his fault, if that's what you're thinking. The place was struck by lightning, but the well in town has gone dry and there wasn't no water to put it out. Mr. Horn just stood there in the street along with the rest of us, watching it burn."

"Where can I find him?"

"I'll write down the address and leave it in the kitchen."

"Thank you, Mrs. Trench. I'm sorry this position didn't suit you."

She shrugged. "It's all right, milord. I've never liked cooking much, to be honest. I'm actually a laundress by trade."

PHILIP'S first order of business was to set another work crew the task of drilling a new well. Afterward, he went to the address Mrs. Trench had given him—a boarding house within walking distance of town. He waited in the parlor while Mr. Horn was summoned, and at length a tall thin man appeared. His clothes, skin, and hair were so crisp, Philip expected him to rustle as he walked.

"Mr. Horn? I'm Lord Philip Butler, and I understand you are a very fine cook."

A nod. "I studied the culinary arts in Paris before working at Brown's Hotel, Mayfair, from its inception until last year. Since then, I managed my own restaurant here in town before it was destroyed by fire."

Philip winced at the mention of the fire. "I'm dreadfully sorry about that. I'm addressing the issue about the well as we speak."

"Your presence in Grovebrook has been desperately needed. More than one soul was glad to see the back of Mr. Pratt."

"As was I. Mr. Horn, might you consider working for me as my cook at the manor house? Your accommodations are included, of course, and since I'm the only one in residence at the moment, your duties would be rather light."

"I'm afraid not."

A stab of disappointment. "I see. I'm sorry to have wasted your time."

"You misunderstand me, milord. I'm not interested in the position of cook, but I would consider the position of head butler. I've been in management longer than I was a cook and I've grown used to running things."

Philip's eyebrows rose. "I *am* in need of a butler, but unless you and I are to starve to death, I must have a cook."

"If I may be so bold as to propose another candidate? Mr. McTavish was my chef at the restaurant, but after the fire he went to Leeds to seek employment. I'll send for him forthwith. Until he arrives, I'll gladly undertake the duties of cook as well as butler. It shouldn't be more than a few days."

The weight on Philip's shoulders lifted somewhat. "I'm very much obliged, sir."

He left the boarding house several minutes later, having

extracted his new butler/cook's promise to be available that afternoon. His successful employment of Mr. Horn unexpectedly brightened Philip's mood. Despite the older man's starchy demeanor, he exuded quiet, likable competence. In addition, Philip was looking forward to the regular presence of another human being at Constance Hall.

When he returned home, he discovered two letters that further lightened his heart. One was a letter from Augustus, and the other was from Prudence.

WHILE THE BROUGHAM was being loaded with Kitty's trunks, Ivy kissed her good-bye and touched her cheek with her fingertips.

"You haven't filled out quite as much as I would have liked over the last week, but it can't be helped."

"It wasn't from lack of trying," Kitty said. "I've never eaten so much rich food in my life."

"Well, take every opportunity to put on weight. No man likes a scrawny wife."

"Yes, Grandmama."

"And if there are any disagreements between you and Philip, don't expect to run back here to me."

Ivy's brief smile indicated her statement was said in jest, but Kitty was so anxious about seeing her husband again she was in no mood to laugh.

"Yes, Grandmama."

She climbed into the carriage, hoping her trembling wasn't visible to Bridget. The maid had never been the talkative sort, fortunately, so during the drive Kitty was left to her own conflicted thoughts. On the one hand she longed to see Philip… so very fervently. On the other hand, she dreaded facing him. Devising an apology seemed easy enough, but she simply couldn't predict his reaction. *I must take things as they come and pray I find the right words. Our marriage is worth fighting for, and I mustn't let him slip away.*

The morning was beautiful, albeit a trifle warm, and the roads were good. Less than an hour later, the brougham passed a beautiful stonework and metal sign announcing the entrance to Grovebrook. To Kitty's eye, the marker appeared to be new, and she suspected it had been built at Philip's direction. As the carriage rolled into town, she gazed out the window with keen interest. Several workmen were making repairs to various shops and buildings, and although the pretty little town showed evidence of neglect, it was clear a restoration was underway.

As they drove through the town and across a small bridge, Kitty knew it would not be too much longer until the carriage reached the manor house. Doubts began to crop up like mushrooms after a heavy rain. Should she have sent word of her arrival beforehand? What if Philip refused to see her? Perhaps she should have asked Augustus to intervene on her behalf.

The carriage turned off the main road and passed through a set of wrought iron gates next to a gate house. As they drove up the long curving driveway, Bridget spoke at last.

"The manor house is lovely."

The tranquil and picturesque beauty of the Elizabethan structure brought a smile to Kitty's lips. "You're quite right. It really is lovely."

"Lord Philip will certainly be glad you've come."

"Yes." *Let us hope so.*

The brougham stopped in front of the entranceway, but no footmen or servants appeared. Kitty's mouth went dry with fear as she stepped down from the carriage and rang the bell. As she waited, her gaze was drawn to the nameplate affixed to the stone facing. Constance Hall. *Philip named the house after me! He cannot hate me so very much then...can he?* At length, an immaculately attired butler answered the door.

"Welcome to Constance Hall. May I ask who is calling?"

"I'm Lady Philip. I apologize for the appalling lack of notice, but will you inform my husband I've arrived?"

PHILIP BLOTTED the ink on his accounting ledger, sat back, and took a deep breath. The addition of Mr. Horn to his household had proven to be a godsend. The new cook he'd recommended had arrived and settled in beautifully. In addition, Horn had procured an experienced housekeeper, Mrs. Boyle. The woman had brought a maid with her, so his skeleton staff was coming along. Horn was even interviewing footmen candidates later that afternoon. On a less happy note, his advertisement for a man of business had located few qualified candidates, and his need was becoming dire. Rents from his tenants would be soon due at the first of the month, and he had no one to collect them. If he didn't have income, he'd be obliged to sell more furniture to stay afloat. Already, several rooms had been completely emptied.

Horn appeared in the doorway of Philip's study. "Excuse me, milord, but Lady Philip has arrived."

If the man had done a backflip, Philip could not have been more astonished. "What did you say?"

"Your wife apologized for giving no notice. I've shown her into the drawing room."

Philip stood so abruptly, he nearly knocked over the ink pot. "Horn, I'm without a valet at the moment. H-How do I look?"

"If I may suggest you don your jacket?"

"Oh, yes. Yes, of course."

"And, if I may be allowed to retie your cravat?"

"I'd be quite grateful."

With an impassive expression, the butler crossed over to render his assistance.

"Shall I ask Mrs. Boyle to prepare rooms for Lady Philip?"

Nonplussed, Philip was unsure how to answer. "I don't…I don't know if she's planning to stay."

"She arrived with a large number of trunks and a lady's maid, sir."

"Then, yes. Prepare the best room for her and find accommodations for her maid. Her name is, um, Bridget, I believe."

"Very good, milord."

The butler bowed and departed, leaving Philip to collect himself. Over three weeks had passed since the wedding. Why had Kitty come here, and what did she expect of him? Well, it did no good to speculate. *I never thought I would see her again, and yet here she is.* His impulse was to drop to his knees and send up a prayer of thanks for his deliverance. But in the next breath, he prayed for the strength to keep Kitty at arm's distance.

As he opened the drawing room doors and stepped inside, several discordant notes from the corner piano reached his ears. Kitty stood when she saw him. They regarded one another for several long moments.

"The piano is out of tune," she said.

"I don't think it's been touched for many years. I'll have to have it looked at."

Another painful silence.

"Will you be staying long?" he asked.

"I'm sorry."

"I said, will you be—"

"No, I meant that I apologize."

When Kitty moved out from behind the piano, he was shocked at how thin she'd become. Had she been ill?

"I was completely and utterly wrong to insinuate you had anything to do with Violet Haver," she said.

"You did more than insinuate."

"Yes, you're right. I misspoke just now. Juliet told me she was responsible, albeit accidentally, for revealing our secret to Miss Haver. You can guess the rest. And when Papa told me you'd refused my dowry, I could have died from shame. I know it's too much for you to forgive me right away, but I'd like the chance to prove myself."

Kitty's arrival was stirring up his emotions, and he wasn't exactly sure how they would ultimately sort themselves out. His initial stunned panic had given way to a bittersweet relief, but underneath it all was anger, mistrust, and a great deal of resentment.

"Why?"

She appeared to be taken aback. "I don't understand."

"You're a financially independent woman, Kitty. You're free to go anywhere and do anything. Why would you come to Grovebrook and associate yourself with a man who is, as you put it, beneath you?"

Her translucent skin grew even paler. "I deserve that." The pooling moisture in her eyes made them gleam. "After much painful introspection, I've concluded you're a far better person than I am. I'm proud to be your wife."

"Not good enough."

"I was afraid!"

"Of what? Of me?"

"Yes." She averted her eyes. "Of m-marriage."

Her blush and expression revealed her meaning more than her words ever could.

"But you're not anymore?"

She gulped. "I'm here because I love you, Philip."

The words seemingly hung in the air but failed to melt the ice around his heart. Her apology seemed to be heartfelt and sincere, but after everything that had passed between them and the torture he'd endured at her hands, could he forgive and forget so easily? No. He'd given his heart away to her too soon in the recent past, and he was unwilling to let his guard down now.

"You've a peculiar way of showing it." He crossed over to the bell pull and gave it a tug. "I'll assemble the staff and introduce you to them formally."

~

SHORTLY AFTER KITTY met the staff, the butler announced lunch. Despite her lack of appetite, she vowed to finish everything set in front of her. As she and Philip were seated, she stole a glance at him. Dark smudges were visible under his eyes, but it was his change of demeanor which was the most noticeable. Before the wedding, he'd been generally sunny and cheerful. Over the course of three short weeks, he'd become guarded and wore an air of sadness like a cloak. Although she longed to hold him and kiss his melancholy away, she knew her caresses were not yet welcome. He hadn't accepted her apology, exactly, but he had at least allowed her to make one. What came next?

"Have you heard anything from Prudence?" she asked.

"I had a letter several days ago. She and Kirkham are well and have been living in Scotland, but I sent a message urging them to come here. I've also heard from Augustus. It's as I feared; Trestlebury has cut his daughter off financially and pronounced me unwelcome in his house."

"Oh, no. Poor Prudence. Does Kirkham have any prospects?"

"Not of which I am aware."

Kitty cast about for another, safer topic. "As I drove through town, I noticed many improvements are underway. I assume they are your doing?"

"Yes. I was obliged to discharge the man who had the management of Grovebrook. Among his other deficiencies, his neglect of the town was almost criminal. Unfortunately, I'm having difficulty replacing him."

"Have you considered offering the position to Kirkham?"

Philip's reserved manner slipped. "Why, no, but that would solve a very pressing problem for me. Kitty, that's brilliant! I'll send him an offer straightaway." His transient smile warmed her heart. "I mustn't get my hopes up, of course, but there's a good chance he would accept. The position even includes a cottage for him and Prudence. Why didn't I think of it before?"

"You've had a great many things on your mind. Now that I'm here, I'd like to help in any way I can."

"As a matter of fact, several neighbors have left calling cards, but I haven't had the time to respond."

"I'd be delighted to call on the neighbors on your behalf. I don't have proper calling cards yet, but I wouldn't want to wait. I'll just write my name on one of yours until I get new ones."

She answered Philip's smile with one of her own, but the gesture had the opposite effect from what she'd intended. Although he thanked her, it was as if a mask descended over his features and his manner turned cool. Kitty was hurt, but she tried to see the silver lining in the clouds. Even if it was just for a moment, she'd managed to break through his defenses. With persistence, patience, and a little luck, she would pull the wall down between them forever. She removed her Claddagh ring and put it on the tablecloth between them.

"I won't yield until we're friends again."

Several emotions flitted across Philip's face as he stared at the ring. He picked it up, reached for her hand, and slid the ring back into place.

"I wouldn't want you to."

EVERY NEW DAY presented another opportunity for Kitty to prove herself worthy of Philip's trust. Although the awkward silences became fewer, the gulf between them remained. Their former easy manner with one another had disappeared, and she didn't know how to regain it. Seemingly a lifetime ago, she'd been confident in her ability with men, but now she was at a complete loss. Ivy had pushed hard to make sure she'd recovered a semblance of physical attractiveness, but Philip seemed oblivious.

In the absence of anything else, Kitty settled for being as helpful as possible. As they strolled in the garden before dinner one evening, he mentioned his lack of a valet.

"I would have liked to hire someone local, but nobody qualified wants the job."

"Why don't you send for your previous valet?" she suggested. "I'm sure your father wouldn't mind."

"You don't suppose Henry would rail at leaving a grand estate to work for me, do you?"

"You're the lord of the manor now, Philip! I would imagine he would consider it a great honor."

As he regarded her, the tension around his eyes eased and he chuckled.

"What?" she asked.

"It's just that being referred to as the lord of the manor feels…rather splendid."

She smiled. "I think the lord of the manor should invite Grovebrook's mayor and his wife to dinner. It would be good politics to discuss all your changes and future plans with local leaders, don't you suppose? You don't want to inadvertently put anyone's nose out of joint."

A look of surprise. "The thought hadn't occurred to me."

"I'll issue an invitation to dinner when I call on the mayor's wife tomorrow afternoon. I also think I should call on the wives of your farming tenants."

"Why?"

"After so many years of neglect, there may be old grievances that need to be aired out. I'll introduce myself and hopefully smooth things over. After all, a happy tenant pays his rent promptly."

For the first time in a long while, Philip's smile was unrestrained. He pulled Kitty into an embrace, but almost as quickly let her go.

"Oh, Philip, don't push me away. It feels so good to be in your arms again."

"I'm sorry. This isn't easy for me."

In the next moment, he traced a path down her cheek with his fingertips. She closed her eyes, leaned into the caress, and murmured his name. Unfortunately, footsteps interrupted the moment and Philip's hand dropped to his side.

"I beg your pardon, milord, but dinner is served."

As Kitty accompanied Philip into the house, she swallowed her disappointment. She'd been almost certain he'd meant to kiss her. Although she was encouraged by the progress she'd made, perhaps it was time to play the coquette.

From then on, it became a game how far she could go without getting caught. Her skills as a flirt came in useful, when the art of deliberately displaying an ankle or the curve of her décolletage appeared to be accidental. Her efforts seemed to be working. Their conversations were growing more intimate, and she found Philip's gaze increasingly resting on her face. Occasionally, when he thought she wasn't looking, she caught his eyes roaming down her body. Although they were married, it still felt as if she were engaging in something scandalous. Each night she'd wondered if he would come to her, but he hadn't. Would Philip ever make her a proper wife?

GOOD COMPANY

One afternoon, about a month after Kitty arrived, the butler announced a pair of very welcome visitors to Constance Hall. As Philip and Kitty entered the drawing room, they discovered Kirkham and Prudence in a passionate embrace. Although the two newlyweds sprang apart immediately, there was no trace of apology in their demeanor.

Kirkham and Philip shook hands and slapped each other on the back. Kitty gave Prudence a kiss on the cheek.

"We're so glad you've come, and we insist you stay at Constance Hall as long as you like," Kitty said.

"We're very grateful for your hospitality, I can assure you," Prudence said.

The woman's appearance was so transformed, she was almost unrecognizable from the girl Kitty had known in London. The simplicity with which she was arranging her hair flattered her features far more than the complicated arrangements devised by her former lady's maid. In addition, her relaxed demeanor and obvious happiness lent Prudence a charm she'd never exhibited before. She had become beautiful.

"You're looking very well, Prudence," Kitty said. "Marriage quite agrees with you."

"Indeed it agrees with us both!" Kirkham picked his wife up in his arms and twirled her around.

Prudence shrieked with laughter. "Put me down! You'll have our friends thinking we've lost our minds."

"I have lost my mind," Kirkham declared. "I'm mad in love with you."

Tears stung the backs of Kitty's eyelids and she found herself feeling envious. *If I hadn't put my foot in it, Philip and I could have been this happy.* She stole a glance in his direction, and his expression was sad. A lump formed in her throat, but she shook it off.

"Come, let's show you to your rooms," she said. "Dinner is at seven."

Kirkham raised his glass of wine at dinner. "I propose a toast to the fortunate husbands of these two beautiful women."

Philip raised his glass. "Cheers."

Prudence giggled and exchanged a pleased glance with Kitty.

"Well, now that we're here, Butler, I hope you don't mind if we talk a little business. I was intrigued by the offer of employment in your last letter," Kirkham said. "When do I start?"

A grin. "You accept? How simply marvelous!"

Relief flowed through Kitty. "What wonderful news! Let's drive to town after breakfast tomorrow, Prudence, so you can see your new residence."

Prudence clasped her hands together in delight. "I can't wait!"

"I warn you, it's not nearly as grand as Trestlebury House, but it does have its own apple orchard," Philip said. "Hopefully the fruit hasn't all been scrumped by now. I gave permission to one of the local lads to help himself."

"I adore apples," she said. "We can press our own cider!"

"You'll need a cook and a housekeeper," Kitty said. "Come with me when I call on the mayor's wife tomorrow afternoon. Perhaps she'll have some suggestions for you."

"How kind you are, Kitty! I like it so much better in the country than in town. I feel as if we can be ourselves at long last, instead of acting the way everyone else wishes we were."

"I thought I'd miss London far more than I have." Kitty's gaze rested on her husband. "It helps when you're in good company."

"Hear, hear," Kirkham exclaimed.

Kitty gave Philip a smile. "I've had an idea. What do you say to throwing a party in a month's time? We'll invite the local gentry and prominent townsfolk. Perhaps I can induce Grandmama to attend."

"I've no objection," Philip said. "Hopefully it will be the first of many celebrations at Constance Hall."

"Naming the manor house after Kitty was a stroke of brilliance. I think we should name the cottage, too." Kirkham waggled his eyebrows at his wife. "How does Prudence Place sound?"

She grimaced. "Don't you dare! I've always detested the name Prudence anyway, and wouldn't like to see it memorialized on a building. I think we should call it Cousin's Cottage."

"I love it," Kirkham said. "What a charming idea."

Prudence and Kirkham continued to flirt and tease one another the remainder of the evening. Although it was delightful to see the couple so happy, Kitty felt excluded. From the set of Philip's mouth, she could tell he felt the same way.

After everyone had retired that night, she yearned for him to visit her bedroom and finish what they'd started in the carriage after the wedding. She read a book by candlelight, hoping he would be encouraged by the light underneath her door. Finally, when her eyelids began to droop, she accepted the fact he wasn't coming and blew out the flame.

PHILIP PACED IN HIS BEDROOM, sleepless and frustrated, willing his desire for his wife to ebb. He longed for her as never before, but he was determined to stay the course. He was not insensible to her efforts to beguile him, but since she'd confessed her fear of marriage—the marriage bed more specifically—he vowed she should come to him. Only then could he be sure she was completely ready to be his wife. Although his body wished it were otherwise, he would not make any efforts to seduce or cajole her...no matter how much it was tearing him apart. Finally, at midnight, he bent over his washbasin and soaked his head with a pitcher of cool water. As dribbles ran down the exposed skin of his chest, he experienced only a slight relief. Unable to bear it any longer, he shrugged off his dressing gown, pulled on some clothes, and left the house. Perhaps if he walked until he dropped from exhaustion, he could sustain his resolve.

PRUDENCE AND KITTY roamed through Cousin's Cottage the following morning, pulling dusty sheets from furniture and examining every nook and cranny. Although the closets weren't overly large, and the place was in need of cleaning, Prudence pronounced it perfect in every way.

"There's even a place for a spinning wheel in the corner. It's going to be such fun to spin when it's sheep shearing season. I understand several of the local farmers raise wool."

"I believe you're right. I'm glad you like the place. You can walk to Grovebrook from here quite easily."

"I wonder if Kirkham would like to move in tomorrow? I adore being alone with him." She giggled. "I don't suppose with the way we've been carrying on it will be too much longer before babies are on the way…if it hasn't happened already."

Kitty's cheeks warmed. "I confess, I'm envious of your happiness."

Prudence cocked her head. "I don't mean to pry, but I did notice something has changed between you and Philip. It's none of my business, of course, but I'm a very good listener if you'd like to talk."

With a forlorn sigh, Kitty sank down on a dusty sofa. "I hurt him badly, Prudence. I sent him away after the wedding breakfast and we never became a proper couple. We're trying to work things out now, but progress has been slow."

"Do you mean you've not…?"

A shake of the head.

"Oh, Kitty, you simply must! I can assure you, it will make all the difference in the world."

"I've been hoping he would come to me, but so far he hasn't." Her skin was so flushed with embarrassment, it prickled painfully.

"You must go to him. Tonight wouldn't be too soon."

"But—"

"If you're nervous, gulp down a glass of strong spirits before you go in."

"What if he sends me away?"

Prudence laughed. "He won't send you away. You bruised his ego before, and he needs to know you want him. Men are rather basic creatures, when it comes right down to it."

"You think so?"

"I know so. I'll tell you a secret; before I saw how you and Philip loved each other, I was a little afraid of marriage. It was your relationship that inspired me to elope with Kirkham, and I can never thank you enough."

The tight band around Kitty's chest eased. "Tonight, then."

~

DESPITE GOING about her duties that afternoon, Kitty's mind was miles away. When she was chatting with the mayor's wife, she was thinking about Philip. When she and Prudence were browsing through the shops in town, she found herself hoping he would ride by on his horse. Philip's presence was so distracting at tea, she almost forgot to eat the lovely cake Mr. McTavish had made. Her thoughts toward her husband were so scandalously wicked, in fact, she blushed at almost everything. She had to give herself a shake before everyone began to think her daft.

When dressing for dinner that night, she donned her lowest neckline, pleased to see she was no longer in need of padding to fill out the bodice. There was no disguising Philip's glance of appreciation when she appeared. Over his shoulder, she could see Prudence stifling a giggle. Kitty made sure to touch Philip at every opportunity and to gaze at him across the dinner table. When Prudence was playing the newly tuned piano afterward, Philip stood nursing a snifter of brandy next to the fireplace. Kitty crossed over, took his arm, and pressed herself as close to him as possible. He showed no visible reaction, but a flush spread up from his collar.

After everyone retired, Kitty retrieved the nightdress she'd purchased for her trousseau and slipped it over her head. As she examined her reflection in the looking glass, the sheer fabric of the gown made it seem as if she were wearing nothing at all. For modesty's sake, she brought her hair over her shoulder to cover her bodice, but then shook her tresses back away from her face. Tonight wasn't the time for modesty, but to prove to Philip how much she loved him.

As a precaution against nerves, she'd smuggled the bottle of brandy to her room. When she poured several inches of the amber liquid into a glass, her hands shook so much that some of the brandy spilled onto the table. She took a long drink and immediately regretted it. The fiery liquid brought tears to her eyes and made her cough. At least after she'd composed herself, the trembling had stopped. As Kitty picked up her wrapper, her door opened without warning. When Philip appeared, clad in a dressing gown, her heart skipped a beat.

"Hullo there, sir. I believe you have me at a disadvantage."

He gave her a meaningful glance before turning the key in the lock. "Let's hope by morning I'll have remedied the situation."

She let her wrapper fall to the floor, followed closely by her night rail. Philip's gasp of appreciation sent a flush of pleasure to her cheeks and made her glad she'd gained back her weight.

"You're completely beautiful, Kitty."

Moments later, she was in her husband's arms, and he was kissing her like a starved man. His lips trailed down her neck. "The thought of you has been driving me wild and I can stay away no longer."

"I wanted you to come so badly. I was just on my way to your room."

Philip pulled back long enough to gaze into her eyes. "You've no idea how much I adore you."

She arched against him. "I can't wait for you to show me."

In one smooth motion, he scooped her up off her feet and carried her toward the bed. As Kitty reveled in his strength, his desire became hers and all fear faded away. And she was in bliss.

Dear Juliet,

My heart is full to bursting with joy! I cannot begin to tell you how wonderful married life is when you're with the man you love. I urge you to never settle for anything less, so you can be as happy as I am.

Prudence and Kirkham have moved into Cousin's Cottage and are terribly good together. If anyone harbors any doubts about the sagacity of their union, they should do so no longer. I've never seen a couple so beautifully made for one another...unless it's Philip and myself! Prudence has blossomed into a very handsome woman, and I think it must be the love her husband showers upon her daily.

As Philip's new man of business, Kirkham has been doing a splendid job and the tenants all like him very much. We are approaching the harvest season and are planning to host a festival in the town afterward to celebrate.

Now that the London Season is winding down, I urge you to come visit, whenever you like and for as long as you wish. Philip and I would simply adore it if you could be here for our first Christmas at Constance Hall.

Very Truly Yours,

Kitty

Just as Kitty had sealed her letter, Philip stuck his head in the library. "There you are!" He crossed over to give her a long, lingering kiss, and then picked her up in his arms, carried her to the sofa, and settled her on his lap. "I've been missing you cruelly all morning."

As she put her arms around her neck, tears pricked the back of her eyelids. Philip frowned. "Is something amiss?"

Kitty shook her head. "I'm just so gloriously happy."

"As I am, my love."

"Will we always be this happy, do you suppose?"

"No."

"What?"

He grinned. "I daresay we'll be even happier with every passing day."

They kissed.

RAKE & ROMANCE

Juliet's plans to wed Lord Elbourne come to naught when she discovers he's obliged to wed an heiress instead. To salvage her dignity, she enters into a ruse with the heiress's brother, whom she views as a rake. Unfortunately, he's also the most attractive man she's ever met.

Cody Gryphon will do anything to see his sister Stephanie wed to Lord Elbourne, including entering into a temporary engagement with her romantic rival. Although he intends to return to Texas as soon as his sister is wed, he finds it increasingly difficult to resist Juliet's charms.

Can a rake and a debutante find their happily ever after?

Keep reading for an excerpt...

EXCERPT FROM RAKE & ROMANCE

Late July 1845. London, England

As the carriage rolled through the streets of London at a brisk clip, Juliet and her mother were obliged to hang on to the straps overhead to avoid sliding to the floor. When one of the wheels hit a particularly large bump, Mrs. Beaucroft made a sound of disgust.

"This is your father's fault, you know. I can't believe he kept the carriage out so late this afternoon, especially when he knew you and I had been invited to a soirée."

"We're only a little late for the party, Mama. If it was that important to you to arrive on time, we could have hired a carriage."

"Nobody who's anybody arrives to a party in a hired carriage, dear." A smile replaced the frown. "When you're Lady Elbourne, I daresay you'll have your pick of carriages."

"Mama, I beg you not to go on about that. Augustus and I get on together swimmingly, but he's given me no indication he's about to propose."

Mrs. Beaucroft seemed to pay her no heed. "I'm rather vexed

at him, I must say. We've very few social events left in the Season, and he's not even going to be at the soirée tonight."

"Since his papa summoned him home, it's hardly his fault. I do hope nothing's wrong."

"Lord Moregate would have said something in his message if anything had been terribly wrong."

"I suppose so."

"At any rate, if Augustus doesn't propose soon, we'll have very little time to revel in your triumph before the Season ends."

Juliet made no response other than to stare out the window. If truth be told, she partly agreed with her mother. Although she wasn't at all annoyed with Augustus, she *was* looking forward to becoming engaged to the most eligible bachelor of the Season. Wouldn't all the naysayers who said she couldn't hold a candle to her sister get their comeuppance! In addition, the gown she was wearing that evening was a particular favorite of hers, and she was disappointed the earl wouldn't have the chance to see it. The darts in the white silk bodice made her waist look exceptionally small, and the cornflower blue embroidery on the full overskirt went well with her porcelain complexion and toffee-colored hair. Oh, well, perhaps she could wear it for him another time.

At Lord and Lady Ayscoghe's soirée, Juliet left Mrs. Beaucroft chatting with a gaggle of matrons and went in search of someone her own age. The gathering was filled with all manner of pleasant and well-heeled company, but she suddenly felt the absence of her sister more keenly than ever before. Kitty had been her near constant companion all her life, so Juliet had almost never been alone. Her sister had married recently, however, and was living with her new husband, Lord Philip, in the country. Philip's elder brother, Augustus, could usually be relied upon for amiable conversation, but he was absent tonight. Perhaps it was *his* comforting presence she missed most of all.

Before Juliet had gone more than a few steps, Lady Lovejoy

descended. As usual, the widowed countess was clad in an exquisite couture gown of the finest materials, undoubtedly acquired during one of her frequent jaunts to Paris.

"Come with me, my dear. I've something I must speak with you about."

The countess maneuvered her into an alcove, where they had a modicum of privacy.

"First of all, I've have had it from very good sources that your former friend, Miss Haver, is completely ruined to all good society."

The way the woman said the word *ruined* left absolutely nothing to the imagination, and Juliet was dismayed. "Are you quite sure?"

"Her parents have disowned her, and there can be no more reliable confirmation than that."

Since Violet Haver had tried to interfere with Kitty's courtship, Juliet had several excellent reasons for holding a grudge. Nevertheless, she wasn't so hard-hearted as to rejoice in her misery.

"I'm dreadfully sorry to hear it. Despite Violet's missteps, I don't wish her ill. I suppose her ruination is Lord Gryphon's doing?"

"You've supposed correctly. That knave has been responsible for the downfall of more than one foolish girl, although usually not a girl as highly placed as Miss Haver. He's such a reprobate, nobody will receive him any longer. In fact, his grandfather, Lord Harkencester, is so disgusted with that entire branch of the family, he's decided to settle the estate on his younger son, Lord Horatio."

On that score, Juliet had little trouble believing the countess. Indeed, she held a far less charitable view of Lord Gryphon than she held of Violet and possessed an even larger grudge. The viscount had tried to take liberties with Kitty, and only the timely intervention of Lord Philip had salvaged her reputation.

If Lord Gryphon had been financially and socially disadvantaged, it was because he deserved it.

"Lord Gryphon will still inherit the title of marquess someday, won't he?"

"Yes, but otherwise he's been cut off without a penny. His parents, Lord and Lady Kesselbury, are still received, but Lord Gryphon can find no ready welcome anywhere. It's a sad situation, really."

"And to think, Lord Gryphon once sought Kitty's hand in marriage!"

"Your sister is much better off where she is, despite her rather unconventional courtship with Lord Philip. At any rate, this brings me to my request. Lord Horatio has just returned to England with the goal of getting his daughter married off. He's been living in Texas these past seventeen years and made a vast fortune of his own in cattle."

Juliet was impressed. "How very clever of him."

"Yes, it's never easy for a second son to make his way in the world. Lord Horatio is looking for a London home, but in the meantime, he and his family are staying with me. Will you take his daughter under your wing so she has at least one friend in town? I'd consider it a personal favor."

Although she managed to keep her countenance, Juliet's heart sank. She'd rather throw herself into a thorny rose bush than have anything to do with Lord Gryphon's relatives, but she wouldn't dream of saying so. "Why, I'd be glad to befriend Miss Gryphon. I was just thinking how lonely it is for me without Kitty around."

"I knew you'd be willing to help. Miss Gryphon is an attractive girl, apart from her dreadful foreign accent and manners. Unfortunately, she's been unfairly tainted by association with her notorious cousin. If you and I befriend her, however, the stain may be somewhat ameliorated."

Although Juliet smiled, she wasn't so sure she agreed. Her

own family would most certainly be appalled by anyone bearing the name of Gryphon. Nevertheless, Lady Lovejoy was an influential member of society, and her requests were rarely refused.

"I'll do what I can, naturally."

"Lord Horatio expects his daughter to make an excellent match, so your alliance with Miss Gryphon will stand you in good stead going forward." The countess giggled. "What am I saying? Considering your close relationship with Lord Elbourne, you're hardly in need of any assistance in society."

Although the implication brought color to Juliet's cheeks, she pretended not to understand. "Indeed, Augustus has been a splendid friend."

"Don't be so modest! All society is awaiting the announcement of your engagement to the earl."

"I hate to disappoint anyone, but no such announcement is forthcoming." Augustus hadn't yet proposed, so Juliet could hardly give any other response. Furthermore, it was better to heighten the suspense by denying the truth of the matter. When she was ready to make the announcement, her triumph would be that much greater. "Is Miss Gryphon here this evening?"

"Yes, but she's playing billiards with the gentlemen."

"No!" Juliet's hands flew to her mouth and her eyes widened in horror.

"I'm afraid so. I suggested she circulate, but she seemed intent on her game."

"Doesn't Miss Gryphon understand the proper way to behave in London society?"

"Alas, her mother perished when the child was only twelve. Lord Horatio assures me his daughter learned all the proper graces at a girls' boarding school in America." She wrinkled her nose. "Only heaven knows what she'll have to unlearn, but I'm sure you'll be an excellent influence."

"I'll do my best."

Despite her assertion, Juliet wasn't entirely sure if her best would be good enough. After all, she'd failed to save poor Violet from disaster. To be fair, however, her former friend had never sought her help.

Lady Lovejoy beckoned. "Come with me and I'll introduce you."

ABOUT THE AUTHOR

Originally from Southern California, Suzanne G. Rogers currently resides in beautiful Savannah, Georgia. She lives on an island populated by exotic birds, deer, and gators.

ALSO BY SUZANNE G. ROGERS

HISTORICAL ROMANCE

<u>Graceling Hall Series</u>

Larken (Book One)*

Lord Apollo & the Colleen (Book Two)

The Vanishing Beauty (Book Three)

<u>The Beaucroft Girls</u>

Ruse & Romance (Book One)*

Rake & Romance (Book Two)*

<u>The Mannequin Series</u>

The Mannequin (Book One)*

Grace Unmasked (Book Two)

The Star-Crossed Seamstress (Book Three)

A Chance of Rayne (Book Four)

The Substitute (Book Five)

<u>The Gilded Age Series</u>

Duke of a Gilded Age (Book One)

Lady of a Gilded Age (Book Two)

<u>Standalone Titles</u>

Spinster

Lady Fallows' Secrets

My Fair Guardian

A Gift for Fiona

Jessamine's Folly

The Ice Captain's Daughter

*Audiobook available

www.ingramcontent.com/pod-product-compliance
Lightning Source LLC
Chambersburg PA
CBHW071319150726
47997CB00002B/523